ORPHAN HUNT

A Pinkerton Justice Novel

Other books by Will Hutchison

- Secrets of the Stones

Pinkerton Justice Series

- The Sins of Serpent's Creek
- Orphan Hunt

The Ian Carlyle Series

- Follow Me to Glory
- The Gettysburg Conspiracy
- Satan's Last Whisper

Non-Fiction

- Artifacts of the Battle of the Little Big Horn: Custer, the 7th Cavalry & the Lakota and Cheyenne Warriors
- Crimean Memories: Artefacts of the Crimean War

ORPHAN HUNT

A Pinkerton Justice Novel

by

Will Hutchison

ORPHAN HUNT

Published by Victory Lane Creative Works
Gettysburg, Pennsylvania.

Printed in the United States of America.
First printing: March 2026.

ISBN 978-1-7368918-2-7

To my loving and ever-tolerant wife,
Rosemary – my muse, my everything.

Chapter 1

The Train

The desert wind howled like a banshee from hell, whipping dust across the empty stretch of track. The Atchison, Topeka, and Santa Fe Railroad train, a massive black beast, thundered through the night toward unknown danger. The train included an engine, a tender, a passenger coach, an express car, a stock car, and a caboose. It moved quickly, given the lack of visibility through the swirling dust. The lone engineer, a tall, lanky man wearing a simple peaked cap and goggles, leaned out of the cab window, trying to see ahead. He was nervously humming his favorite tune, Dixie. He had no idea that around the next bend, railroad ties and fallen trees created a major barrier across the tracks.

Six shadowy figures, sweating from the tension of their long wait, huddled among the scattered piñon pines and junipers beside the tracks. Rifles and shotguns glinted in the pale moonlight. Two mounted desperados kept all six horses a short distance behind the others. The outlaws stood ready to strike once the train slowed to a stop. Their carefully planned obstacle would work for sure. The moment would soon arrive — the moment the gang would get rich. Bandanas covering their faces, each man harbored a secret fear of what was coming.

Their leader, a grizzled outlaw with a menacing grin, growled, “Easy, boys, this here’s gonna be like yer ol’ Ma pluckin’ a chicken fer Sunday eatin.’ And when we’re done fleecin’ these jaspers, we’re gonna have ourselves a time. Yes, sir, we’re gonna hoot and holler.” The others smiled. The tension eased a bit, but still hung in the air like stale cigar smoke.

As the train rounded the bend, a sudden shot rang out. At the same time, the startled engineer saw the obstruction ahead and scrambled back into the cab to apply the brakes. The train whistle shrieked a long, mournful cry, a desperate plea for help that would go unheard in this lonely landscape. The engine came to a complete stop, and the leader of the gang, a Mexican desperado everyone knew as Carlos, led the charge. He and his men, screaming a rebel yell, ran, guns drawn, to the train. Four outlaws jumped quickly onto the open platform at the rear of the passenger car. Two went into the passenger car. The other two, including the gang leader, smashed in the door to the express car behind it. A clattering of boots and shouts echoed through the quiet night.

The folks in the passenger car had begun to react in panic to the gunshot and the abrupt stopping of the train. As the bandits entered the car, two figures, almost unnoticed among the frightened passengers, exchanged a knowing glance. Pinkerton Detective Caleb Tasker and his protégé, Detective Jefferson Cobb, dressed in town coats over work shirts, like ordinary laborers, had been placed on this very train, hired by the railroad to protect against such an occurrence.

The first outlaw, a big man wearing a floppy hat, entered the passenger car and fired his massive Colt Dragoon revolver through the roof of the car. As the sound died away and the smoke cleared, the gunman shouted, “Sit yerselves down, and stay put. If ya move, lessen we ask you to…yer dead. Now we're gonna relieve ya'all of whatever cash, coins, or jewelry ya might have."

His partner, a short, stubby man brandishing two Schofield revolvers, moved next to the first outlaw and stuttered, "Th-that's right. S-Sit there and give us yer g-goods and nobody gets hurt."

The difference in their sizes, the smaller one's staccato outburst, and the fact that the shorter one held two large guns made them an outlandish and comical pair, but nobody was laughing. With the passengers seated and somewhat out of the way, Tasker nodded to Cobb. They were seated in the first row near the front of the car, well away from the outlaws. Tasker sat in the window seat on the right, Cobb on his left.

Tasker whispered, "You think now?"

Cobb said in a quiet voice, "I do."

No warning was given. They knew that might provide the outlaws a chance to shoot – too dangerous in the crowded train car. The Pinkertons rose together, guns already out and aimed toward the rear of the car. The two shots they fired sounded like only one. Tasker's bullet caught the big man square in the chest. He looked quite startled as he fell backward. Cobb's bullet smashed into the little man's face below the right eye. They both hit the floor of the train car together – quite dead.

The two detectives rushed down the aisle to the rear of the car, climbing over the two bodies to make sure they were indeed dead. They took positions on either side of the door between the connecting platform linking the passenger car and the express car. The express car door had been forced open, but it was ajar.

Some of the passengers were stepping into the aisle behind them. Cobb commanded, "Stay by your seats and get down!" The passengers complied, too scared to do much else.

Tasker and Cobb removed the spent cartridges from their revolvers and replaced them with fresh ones. Tasker looked across at Cobb. "You think our shots spooked 'em?" he asked, referring to the train robbers he knew would be inside the express car. "They could be waiting for us."

"Doubt it," Cobb replied. "Likely, they'd think the shots were fired by the two we killed just to scare the folks." Both men were removing the spent cartridges from their revolvers and replacing them with fresh ones.

"Hope yer right," Tasker said.

"Me too."

"Kick the door? It isn't locked."

"My pleasure," Cobb said as he rushed across the platform and kicked open the express car door.

Both men crashed into the car. Tasker went high. Cobb went low. Their guns were aimed forward and cocked. They quickly assessed the scene. The body of the express car guard lay face down on the floor, in a pool of blood. They recognized the gang leader, Carlos, from his wanted poster. He and his partner were caught off guard, bending over a strongbox. Carlos carried a small but deadly Lightning revolver holstered on his right hip. The other, who looked more like a frightened young boy than a desperate outlaw, eyed his Messenger shotgun, propped against the car's wall just a foot away.

Their eyes shifted toward the two lawmen flanking the express car's doorway. Both Pinkertons smiled. The air crackled with tension. The silence was broken only by the nervous shifting of the outlaws, weighing their chances if they decided to fight.

Carlos finally scoffed, "Two lawmen against us and my men outside? Likely, you bit off more than you can chew." Although he looked Mexican, as did his young partner, there was no accent.

"You think?" Tasker said. "I think we'll cut you both down before you can blink. Jefferson?"

"I'll take the boy," Cobb whispered.

Tasker told the outlaw leader, "Your call, Carlos, yank that little girly gun, but one twitch an' you'll be deader than a week-old corpse!"

A tense standoff followed, with the robbers exchanging glances, their bravado fading as the two lawmen kept their unwavering gaze. Suddenly, the nervous young outlaw lunged for his shotgun. Cobb fired once, hitting the man before he could reach his weapon.

Carlos, in shocked surprise at Cobb's cold speed, bent further over, raising his hands well above his head. "Don't shoot! Don't shoot!"

Tasker moved in and cuffed the subdued outlaw, hands behind his back. Cobb searched him for any hidden weapons. He found only a knife with a long, slim blade and tossed it aside. He pulled the Lightning from its holster and tucked it into his belt.

"How many are out there?" Cobb asked.

Carlos, having regained some composure, smirked at Cobb. "Too many," he said.

Cobb hit him squarely across the face with the barrel of his Schofield.

The desperado lost his bravado. "Jus two," he said through a bloody, smashed mouth. "Ho'ding our ho'ses."

"That's more like it," Cobb said.

Tasker asked, "Where are they waiting?"

He responded without hesitation. "Jus' outside." He nodded toward the closed sliding door of the express car.

Tasker turned to Cobb. “If they haven’t skedaddled by now, we might as well open that sliding door and take ‘em.”

“Good a plan as any.”

Carlos was recuffed to a giant trunk. The two Pinkertons moved to the sliding door. Side by side, guns ready, they ratcheted it open. Facing them a few yards away were the last two mounted outlaws, each holding the reins of two horses. One fumbled to draw his gun from its holster, but he had no hope. Tasker shot him twice in the chest, and he toppled from his horse. Before Cobb could take the second man, an explosion to their left lifted him from his horse and threw him to the ground, dead before he landed. The horse whinnied, snorted, and fell on top of the fallen outlaw.

The engineer stood there, holding Cobb’s smoking 12-gauge, double-barreled shotgun, a big grin on his face. “I found this by your seat in the passenger car. Thought it might be handy.” He had given both barrels to the poor desperado from a few feet away. The spread also hit the horse. The other horses, frightened and confused, ran off in all directions.

Tasker turned to Cobb and smiled. “Well, I’d say it was definitely useful. You’d better get your shotgun back before our brave engineer gets any more handy with it.”

Chapter 2

A New Mission

With the help of a few willing passengers, it took three hours to clear the track. The bodies were laid out in the caboose, and Carlos went back to join them, cuffed to a seat. There was a conductor on the train, but he had either been asleep or hiding in the caboose throughout the episode. When he appeared, the Pinkertons assigned him to guard Carlos for the rest of the journey.

The trip from Santa Fe to Silver City still had hours to go before reaching its final destination. Tasker and Cobb returned to their seats in the coach car. When they entered, the passengers gave them an ovation, which only made the lawmen feel embarrassed.

As the train resumed its journey and the applause faded, an elderly gentleman approached the lawmen. He wore a tailored black frock coat, a white wing-collared shirt, and a maroon cravat, accented with a diamond stickpin. His gray hair was neatly styled beneath a fashionable high derby. To complete his look of wealth and refinement, he sported a gray Van Dyke beard and mustache and carried a walnut cane with an ornate silver top.

His overly dapper appearance unsettled Tasker and Cobb, but his friendly smile and warm greeting were disarming.

"Gentlemen, my name is Clarence Pembrook. I want to start by congratulating both of you on how you handled a dangerous situation. I believe that, without your help, passengers might have died, possibly including my family and me."

"Thanks for the kind words, Mr. Pembrook," Tasker said. "We were simply doing what we're paid to do – protecting the passengers and property of the Atchison, Topeka, and Santa Fe Railroad."

"Then you are not government police, marshals, or sheriffs?"

"No, sir. We're Pinkerton men. The railroad is one of the Pinkerton Detective Agency's clients."

"Well, for my purposes, that's even better," Pembrook said.

"How so?" Cobb asked.

"I was genuinely impressed by your skill. You see, I have a mission, a job you might be interested in."

"I'm afraid it doesn't work like that, Mr. Pembrook," Tasker said. "The Pinkerton Agency, through our Chicago office, assigns us work. We don't deal directly with clients. Clients pay Pinkerton, and Pinkerton pays us a salary."

"Certainly, certainly. I understand all of that. It's an easy fix. I should mention that, due to my own choices, I've become an extremely wealthy man. I started with a small silver mine and have since expanded to several more, along with many other profitable ventures. I know William Pinkerton. I even knew his late father. Not intimately, mind you, but I've used his services from time to time. I'm confident we can reach an understanding. But first, you need to believe in this mission. In fact, you must be passionate about the cause you're about to take on. May I introduce you to my family?"

By this point, curious passengers could overhear their conversation. Tasker said, "That's fine, but let's not do this here. Too many ears."

"Express car?" Cobb suggested.

"Yes." Tasker turned to Pembrook. "Please round up your family, sir, and bring them back to the next car. It's empty now and will be more private."

"Excellent. We will see you soon."

Tasker and Cobb moved from the passenger car into the express car. The door was hanging on its hinges, but Cobb managed to close it somewhat as they waited.

A few minutes later, Pembrook entered the express car, accompanied by a well-dressed, portly woman with an inviting smile and a slim, sullen teenage boy with a shock of red hair. The Pinkertons noted that the boy's gaze was fixed on the floor of the car.

Pembrook made the introductions. "Gentlemen, this is my wife, Mavis, and our soon-to-be-adopted son, Michael. Mavis, Michael, these gentlemen are Pinkerton detectives, our saviors from those train-robbing villains. They may be able to help with our quest."

Tasker and Cobb tipped their hats. "Ma'am," they said, almost in unison. Tasker extended his hand to shake Michael's, but the boy deliberately turned away.

"Michael!" Mrs. Pembrook scolded. "Manners."

"Sorry, Ma'am," Michael replied curtly. Though he showed respect for Mrs. Pembrook, he didn't shake Tasker's hand.

"All right, Mr. Pembrook," Tasker said. "Let's start with you telling us what this is all about. I have to admit, your approach is a bit unorthodox."

"I know. I know, but this is an unorthodox situation, and

we're rather desperate." He sat on one of the crates, propping his cane against another. "You see, Michael came to us about a year ago to help around our home. Mavis has trouble with her hands and doesn't get around as well as she used to a few years ago."

Mavis, her hands folded in front of her, nodded. "I merely needed some help. By the way, Michael is sixteen."

"Although he worked hard," Pembrook continued, "Michael was initially cantankerous."

Mavis cut in, "For heaven's sake, Clarence, tell the gentlemen how it was. It took us most of a year to get him to realize we weren't his enemies and weren't going to hurt or cheat him. We had a small dog – a mutt who hung around our kitchen. Michael took to the dog. He named him 'Pickle' because the critter loved them. That crazy mutt broke the ice. After he and the dog got together, Michael began to soften toward us. He gradually became the son we always wanted." She smiled at Michael, dabbing her eyes with a silk handkerchief. Michael smiled back at her.

Clarence Pembrook continued. "We became excessively fond of the boy, as you can see, and I believe he realized we were good people. That's when he confided in us, told us his dreadful story. You see, he was …"

Tasker injected, "I think, Mr. Pembrook, all due respect, Michael is old enough to speak for himself." Tasker wanted to size this boy up before getting any further involved.

"Certainly. Absolutely."

Tasker turned to Michael, who finally met his gaze. "Michael, we'd like to hear what happened to you in your own words."

"Don't know you guys, see. Don't care too much, neither. Sorry, Mr. Pembrook, but the people after me and the ones who got my sister ain't jokin' around. They got their hooks in all over – even the coppers."

"These men saved your life today, Michael," Pembrook said. "I think you can trust them."

Cobb added, "We're not coppers, Michael. We work for a private company and answer only to our bosses and our clients. We're on no other payroll. You can count on that."

"Look, lad," Tasker said, "I get it — you don't trust folks easily, and probably for good reason. I don't trust folks much on first meeting, either. I see you're troubled, but we might be able to help you. You'll have to trust somebody sometime, unless you think you can handle it all by yourself."

A long silence followed. Mrs. Pembrook grabbed her handkerchief, took a deep breath, and covered her mouth. She prayed, "Please, God, please let them help my boy...please."

Michael heard her and lowered his head. When he looked up, he first fixed his gaze on Tasker's eyes, then on Cobb's. He seemed to make a decision. "I've been tryin' it by myself. It jus' ain't workin', so what do you wanna know?"

"Start wherever you want," Tasker said.

"I wanna find my sister. That's what I want. She's just a kid. They're doing awful things to her. She's a kid, and ..." Michael deliberately stopped tears from forming in his eyes.

Tough lad, Tasker thought.

Cobb was thinking the same thing. He said, "Maybe start from the beginning, Michael. What's your sister's name?"

"Abigail," Michael blurted out.

A shocked expression crossed Cobb and Tasker's faces—one they couldn't hide from Clarence Pembrook. "What's wrong?" he asked.

"Never mind," Tasker said sharply. The situation had become much more personal for them. On a job in Serpent's Creek, New Mexico Territory, some time ago, Jefferson

Cobb had fallen in love. Though he had been a Sergeant Major in the 10th Cavalry and highly self-educated, he was also Black and a former slave. She was the daughter of a local shopkeeper with deep-seated prejudices. It was nearly impossible for Cobb and the young lady to be together, but the two lovers were determined to make it work. Then, suddenly, she was brutally killed by a gang of lowlifes. Her name was Abigail. The pain from Cobb's loss still lingered. Tasker had been Cobb's commanding officer in the 10th Cavalry, but more than that, they had become inseparable friends. So the pain was also there for Tasker. If this young girl named Abigail was in trouble, it meant a great deal to Cobb and Tasker to help her.

Tasker finally asked, "Michael, you said they got her? Who, where, and how did they do that?"

"You gotta call me Micky. That's my name. Only Mr. and Mrs. Pembrook and Abigail call me Michael. Nobody else!"

Cobb said, "So, Micky...tell us."

Micky gradually revealed the story, piece by piece, with occasional prompts from the Pinkerton men. He was now sixteen—an old sixteen—and his sister was thirteen. Their last name was Bracken, and he was born in Athens, Georgia. Silas Bracken, his father, had returned from the Civil War in 1865, missing a leg and deeply despondent. He never quite recovered from the South's defeat or from losing his limb.

In 1870, Silas married Micky's mother, a naive young woman from Georgia named Catherine. Micky was born two years later, followed by Abigail two years after that. Burdened with melancholy, Silas Bracken took his own life the same year Abigail was born. He left Catherine Bracken with two children, nearly penniless. She earned a modest living as a part-time seamstress but was not very skilled.

In 1882, Catherine and her children moved to New York City with a man Micky only remembered as "Bart." He was supposed to be Catherine's savior, but Bart was not who he claimed to be. When they arrived, he placed the three of them in a small room in a cheap tenement on Little Water Street at Five Points in Lower Manhattan. The room was divided by blankets hung from the ceiling. There were two beds—one small bed where the children slept and a larger one on the other side of the blankets where Catherine slept. Here, she handled the business Bart brought to her day and night.

Micky remembered the grunts and groans of the faceless men who came to their room to see their mother. Catherine grew increasingly depressed. Micky saw her overwhelmed with shame and disgust. One morning, the children woke to find she was gone. Bart appeared the next day and kicked the children out onto the street without explanation. Rumors spread through Five Points that Catherine was dead, killed by Bart in a fight over money she was supposed to have hidden from him.

The harsh, relentless streets of New York City offered little comfort to ten-year-old Micky and his younger sister. They had to survive, and Micky was quickly growing into a young man. He considered it his solemn duty to shield his little sister from the city's brutal grip. He shined shoes, ran errands, worked as a newsboy, and did everything he could to earn enough for a day-old crust of bread for his sister, often going hungry himself.

One bitterly cold night near Five Points, a gentle-spoken woman with a kind face approached them. Her smile was broad, and her words were sweet. She spoke glowingly of the New York Children's Aid Society. This was an organization Micky had heard about on the street. The word was that it was a good place if you qualified. The woman said they did qualify, especially since they could both read and write. They would be given warm beds and food, and eventually the society would find them loving homes or good-paying jobs in the Far West.

According to the kind woman, the program was called ‘Placing Out’ and was designed for children like Micky and Abigail. She even said they would be in high demand for good homes. Abigail’s eyes sparkled with a brightness Micky hadn’t seen in a long time. He felt suspicious because of their past with Bart, but everything about this well-dressed, friendly woman seemed legitimate. He agreed to go along, holding his sister’s tiny hand as they were led to a building some distance from Five Points. They were well-fed, given a nice room to themselves, and slept warmly for the first time in weeks. The next day, Micky found the door to the room locked. The real nature of the kind woman and her helpers soon became clear. They weren’t benefactors, but jailers, and they had nothing to do with the New York Children’s Aid Society. In fact, they took children from the streets of cities like Chicago and New York and sold them out west to the highest bidder. Many ended up as slave labor or prostitutes.

Micky was feisty and belligerent, while Abigail was submissive. They kept the two together in the hope that Abigail would keep her brother in line. They were taken to a room where a dozen other children their age were waiting. From that point on, there were few days when they weren’t beaten with belts and switches, though they only beat Abigail where it wouldn’t show. The beatings were routine, with no apparent reason. Besides being fed barely enough to stay alive and enduring the usual beatings, Micky was pretty much left alone.

Meanwhile, Abigail was taken away for hours at a time. When she returned, she would stare at the walls and cry. No matter how much Micky tried to find out what they were doing to her, she would shake her head and refuse to speak.

Months later, one morning, they came for him. He fought and struggled. His pleas went unheard. The last time he saw Abigail, she was weeping in a corner of their room as he was dragged away, kicking and screaming her name.

Micky's westward journey was long and difficult. He was loaded onto a train with other boys his age, their hopes fading with each mile. More than a week later, the train reached a dusty town, the land flat and empty for miles. By then, Micky was the only boy left on the train.

Micky was taken by a local named Denton in an old, rickety wagon to a large farm. He was handed over to the owner, a man named Cane. Cane stood over six feet tall, a big, round man with a completely bald head. He had a thick black beard that reached halfway down his chest. Micky thought he was wealthy because the guards he hired and the thugs he befriended treated him with "yes, sir, no, sir" respect. He tipped the guards a handful of coins.

The farm was a place of constant hard work and brutal punishment for Micky. Two things became clear. First, it was a large pig farm where the animals were raised and then sold. Second, he had been sold as a slave to the farmer, Cane. Micky's job was to feed the giant animals, keep them fat for sale, and handle the farm's paperwork.

Marcus Cane, a harsh and unforgiving man, saw Micky as a good-for-nothing and cheap labor, treating him no better than his pigs. The beatings were constant, the food scarce, and Micky's dreams of escaping and finding Abigail were the only things keeping him going. Those dreams became harder to hold onto as Cane surrounded himself with local toughs. In fact, he ran a side scheme: if these toughs, for any reason, needed to get rid of someone, Cane would, for a price, dispose of the bodies by tossing them into the pigpens. Some would even arrive in coffins, which had to be opened so the bodies could be removed. The coffins would then be burned. The hogs would eat everything, leaving no trace.

Micky once tried to escape, running down the road toward town from the farm. Denton, the same guard who had initially brought him to Cane's farm, soon caught up with him. The guard beat him until he couldn't stand and then dragged him back to the farm by a rope.

Cane told him that his sister was still within Cane's reach. If Micky tried to escape again, even if he managed to get away, she would be severely punished, maybe even killed.

After Micky's failed escape, Cane introduced a new punishment. He took away Micky's shoes, and that's when the beatings changed. Cane built a split board with two holes for Micky's ankles, similar to an old-time stock. Either he or Denton used a switch to beat the soles of Micky's feet at night. This made it nearly impossible for him to walk the next day. He could still limp around and do his chores with the pigs, but Cane no longer saw running away as an option for his slave. Though Cane never realized it, his punishment backfired. The beatings on Micky's feet were brutal at first, but over time the soles of his feet toughened and became leathery. So much so that he hardly felt the pain anymore, though he still acted like it hurt terribly.

Time dragged on for Micky, yet nothing changed. He was trapped in relentless hard work and daily beatings. He believed that even if he managed to escape, the cost to Abigail would be too high. Without even the hope of escape, Micky grew increasingly sullen and despairing.

Months later, one evening, Micky was peeling potatoes under the kitchen window of Cane's house. The window had been left open, and he overheard a conversation between Cane and one of the local ruffians about Abigail. Apparently, the ruffian was the one who had taken her to her new owner, a madam at a house of prostitution. He didn't say where, but he laughed about her innocence being stripped away in front of him.

Micky believed Abigail's situation couldn't be much worse. He decided he had to act. Hardened by punishment and strengthened by the farm's brutal labor, he saw his chance one night when Cane was alone at the farm. Micky set fire to the barn. When Cane ran out of his house, panic-stricken toward the barn, Micky waited in the shadows. He hit Cane in the head with a shovel until even his mother wouldn't have recognized him, then ran off.

Micky wandered for weeks, his spirit bruised but unbroken, until fate, in a rare moment of compassion, stepped in. He stumbled upon Clarence Pembrook's estate, where he was offered work and a place to stay. The boy proved hardworking and industrious, with his cleverness and drive shining through the stain of his past. Mrs. Pembrook quickly grew fond of him. She was the one who gave him the means to search for his lost sister.

Micky traveled from town to town, chasing every faint rumor and whispered hope. He spoke with others who had been taken west under similar shady circumstances, hearing stories of hardship, abandonment, and broken promises that mirrored his own experiences. He often met people who remembered the darker side of the 'placing out' movement, sharing tales of children sold as slaves, forced into labor, and subjected to abuse.

As for Abigail, the vastness of the country had swallowed her up. Micky never stopped searching, but over time, his hope became a flickering ember, fueled only by memories of her once-bright eyes and his self-imposed duty to protect her.

Micky again had tears welling in his eyes at the end of his story, but he stubbornly refused to let them fall. He blurted out, "Youse know it all now. I got nowhere left to turn, damn it!"

"Language," Mrs. Pembrook said. Micky bowed his head.

"So that's where we stand today, gentlemen," Mr. Pembrook said. "What do you think?"

"That's quite a story," Tasker said. "Give us a minute."

They moved to the other end of the car and spoke softly. "What do you think, Jefferson?"

"We gotta help, Caleb, if you figure his story is true."

Tasker said, "I'm familiar with the Children's Aid Societies and the placing-out system used to find homes or work here in the West for lost or orphaned children. They mostly do good, but I've also heard horror stories, like the one Micky tells. This kid might be lying, but I don't think so."

"Hell, Caleb, if this kid's lying, I'm a ring-tailed possum."

"Well, I reckon you're not a 'possum, Jefferson...so it's settled."

"It is."

"Now we have to persuade our bosses."

They returned to the Pembrooks and Micky. Tasker said, "Thank you, Micky. I know that was tough. You're right, Mr. Pembrook. Micky deserves to find his sister, and Abigail deserves a childhood… a real childhood."

"So, you'll take the case?" Pembrook asked.

"We can't do that," Tasker said, "much as we might like."

Cobb added, "We can strongly recommend," he said, looking directly at Tasker, "and we will...but it's a Pinkerton decision. It has to come from the top down."

Tasker said, "Better it comes from you to our higher-ups than from us. You'll have to work out client fees and the like if they agree to take the case. We'll tidy up this train robbery affair. You do whatever you can, and we'll be waiting."

"I'll handle this. I'll visit William Pinkerton in person. You'll hear from me soon."

"By the way, Micky," Tasker asked, "do you know the names of any of these so-called aid society jaspers?"

Micky thought for a moment. "Only the guard who brought me to Cane's place, 'cause he hung around there afterward about every day. He was one of the ones who beat me. His name was Denton, Marv Denton. He wore some kind of badge — maybe it said 'Sheriff.'"

"That's interesting...and where was this Cane farm?"

"A few miles west of a town called Socorro."

"That's a place to start if we get the go-ahead," Cobb said.

"It is," Tasker replied.

Chapter 3

The Assignment

"Mr. Pembrook, I need a word with Micky. If you don't mind."

"Of course, of course."

"Micky, let's go outside." They stepped onto the platform between the cars, and Tasker shut the passenger car door.

"Look, lad, if we're going to have any luck finding Abigail, we're gonna need better information to go on."

"Like what?"

"A way to identify her if she were in a group of girls her age: how would she stand out? How old did you say she would be today?"

"Oh...I see what you mean," Micky said. "Well, she'd be thirteen now, a real beauty. Bright red hair, like mine, but long and prettier...and she always looked older than she was." Tasker was taking notes.

"That's good, but what if all the girls her age looked lovely and had red hair? How would I know which one she is?"

Micky was thoughtful. "Hey, I know. She has a faint scar on her left cheek, about this long." He showed Tasker his first finger and thumb about three inches apart. “Once, when we was at Five Points, one of the men was beatin’ our ma—bad. Abigail attacked him from behind like a wild dog—scratched his face somethin’ awful. He pulled a straight razor and cut her cheek. Bart musta heard the ruckus ‘cause he came in. He beat the man terrible and cut ‘em up bad. Too late, though. Abigail was already cut and bleedin’ fierce.”

“That’s good, Micky, right good. How much does the scar show?”

“Show?”

“Yeah, if you were five or six feet away.”

“Well, it got better but still showed through even with powder over it.”

“Which cheek?”

“Left...no right.”

“You sure now?”

“Yeah, her right cheek. She was facing him, and he had the razor in his right hand. Pulled it across her face left to right. I’m sure it was on her right cheek.”

“Good. Anything else you can think of?”

“Naw, I guess not.”

“You’ve done well, lad. It will help a lot. I have a few more…”

Micky interrupted him. “Wait. I jus’ remembered.” He reached down and pulled up his right pant leg, then shoved his cotton sock down to his shoe top. There, on the outside of his right foot, above the ankle bone, were two one-inch scars side by side, forming what looked like the number eleven.

“Is that a number?” Tasker asked.

“Yeah. Bart liked to keep track of his property. He carved the number eleven into my skin with a big damn knife he always carried. Hurt like hell.”

“Are you telling me Abigail has one as well?”

"Yeah. Only hers is the number twelve."

"Glad you remembered, Micky. Thanks."

"Find my sister," Micky said. "Remember, she knows my nickname, Micky, but she always insisted on calling me 'Michael.' Maybe if you find her, you can use that as a sort of code so she'll know you're from me."

"I'll do that. I'll do what I can. I promise," Tasker replied, thinking, *That is, if I can get the bosses to go along.*

The rest of the trip to Silver City was uneventful. Upon arrival, Tasker telegraphed the Albuquerque Pinkerton office but didn't mention the Pembrooks, Micky, or Abigail.

Tasker suggested, "Let's take the next train back to Albuquerque."

"Agreed," Cobb said. "Better to be there in person when the wheels are turning on the Pembrook matter."

"Yep."

In the end, Clarence Pembrook proved too quick for them.

They arrived in Albuquerque a week later and immediately went to the small ranch house they had bought together the previous year, which served as a base from which they could act when needed. The house came with the horses they had been considering buying someday. It featured a tiny stable big enough for two horses and maybe a mule. They also hired Manuel, a local Mexican cook, horse groomer, and handyman. He watched the property while they were gone, and it was always clean and ready for them when they returned.

Not long after they set down their carpetbags in the ranch house, a rider arrived with a telegram. Unusually, it was from William Pinkerton himself, addressed directly to Caleb Tasker and marked *'Urgent – Confidential.'*

It read:

Caleb – Well done on the train. I understand you discussed a new case with Pembrook. It was a bit premature, but no matter. Work with our new client, Clarence Pembrook. Find Abigail and return her, if possible. This will fulfill our obligation to the client. Continue your investigation as a moral duty to me and Brother Robert. Find and eliminate the roots of this abominable organization at all costs, wherever it takes you. Expenses are covered, within reason, of course. Use your Apache if needed. All our resources are available to you. Good luck.

– Will Pinkerton

"If that doesn't beat all," Tasker said, showing Cobb the telegram.

"Easier said than done," Cobb said after reading it.

"Guess old Pembrook was the real thing. He obviously had pull with Will Pinkerton."

"Got him riled up. So, where do we go from here, Caleb? Pick up Sammy? We can always use a long-range shooter, and there's none better than Sammy."

"True, Jefferson. I've been feelin' kinda exposed without our third musketeer to cover our backs."

"The little rascal's well smitten. The Doc's daughter has him roped and branded. He even changed his name to sound more respectable."

Tasker nodded, smiling. "He sent me a telegram. Not our half-Apache Sammy Wolf-Killer anymore. Signed it, Samuel Wolf. Made note that we could still call him Sammy."

"They aren't married yet, but it's only a matter of time."

"It is, Tasker said. "He's in Serpent's Creek with Doc and Savannah right now. I wouldn't want to go tanglefoot with Savannah Abbott."

"Hell no," Cobb said. "She's like a mama bear with a cub. Did you know Sammy's not only taught Savannah to sign but also apparently Doc and everyone around him?"

"Sounds like Sammy. Sending him back East to that school was a good thing in so many ways."

Cobb asked, "So where do we start?"

"I reckon that pig farm outside Socorro. See if we can locate this jasper, Denton. Might be we need a few words with him. We can see about Sammy after we talk to Denton."

"This Denton. He's supposed to be some kind of law."

"We'll see."

"Train, stagecoach, or horseback?"

"Let's pick up our new horses from the livery and head out at our own pace. We might need to take a less-traveled route, and riding horses will give us the flexibility to do so. Should only take a few days."

"I like it when all that West Point training comes through, Caleb."

"Go suck a snake, Sergeant Major Cobb, a mean one," they both laughed.

Later that day, Tasker and Cobb stopped by the Albuquerque office to visit an old friend, Buford Cartwright. "Buford," Tasker greeted him, "are you still tied into most every establishment of ill repute from Chicago to California?"

"Not even a greeting or by-your-leave? I'm crushed."

"Howdy, Buford," Cobb said. "How the hell you been?"

"Oh. Yeah," Tasker added, smiling. "Greetings and by your leave. Will that do?"

"That's much better, and by the way… You owe me a few pours of a fine whiskey for that thing in Serpent's Creek and after."

"I do. I do. Well… do you?"

"Do I what?"

"Do you still have your ear to the ground?"

Cartwright, a man of considerable girth, served as the Pinkerton Agency's information-gathering specialist west of Chicago. He maintained remarkably accurate sources across the West and had often proved a valuable asset to the detectives. Preferring to work from his desk in the office, he had no desire to go into the field. All his connections were made through the telegraph system or word of mouth.

"In answer to your question, Mister Tasker, nothing happens in those dens of debauchery that old Buford doesn't know about or can't find out. What do you need?"

"It's a long shot, my friend, even for you," Tasker said.

"The hell you say. Sounds right up my tree."

Cobb said, "Caleb's right, Buford. This one is a prickly pear if ever there was."

"Fine. Let's have it."

Tasker reported meeting the Pembrooks and hearing Micky's story. "We received word from above that we are to pursue the case, find the sister, and destroy this organization. No small task."

"But a worthy one, I reckon," Cartwright said. "What do you need from me? I guess you know I'll do whatever it takes to help."

"I figured that," Tasker said. He gave Cartwright a description of Abigail, including her name, red hair, scars, number twelve, and all the details.

"Likely not using her real first name, maybe 'Abby,'" Cobb added. "Like Caleb said – a long shot."

"Hmmm," said Cartwright. "I like a challenge. I'll put feelers out as far as I can reach. Maybe we'll get lucky."

"That's all we can ask, Buford, and thanks. Cobb and I will be grateful."

"That you will. Now let's go have a drink. I'm

parched—and hungry."

"Maybe next time, Buford, we gotta rustle up our horses and pack for the trip," Tasker said.

"Next time, my butt? If I find your girl, you might owe me a whole damn case of whiskey."

"That's a deal," Tasker said.

Typically, Tasker and Cobb rented horses as needed, depending on where their assignments took them. It was more convenient than putting them in a stock car on a train or towing them behind a stagecoach. However, a few months ago, after buying their ranch house in Albuquerque and its small stable, they were offered the chance to acquire excellent mounts at a very low price.

Tasker chose an Appaloosa because he preferred the Nez Perce Indian breed. It was roan-colored and leopard-spotted. He named it 'Blaze' after its reddish hue and the fierce, burning look in its eyes.

Cobb rode Morgans for the twenty years he spent in the 10th Cavalry, and he loved them for their kind nature and intelligence. This time, however, he chose a stunning buckskin mare, light brown with a black tail and mane. The horse had two white socks on its front legs, extending over the fetlocks. The brown matched Cobb's skin perfectly, and the black matched the hat, town coat, vest, trousers, and boots he always wore. Together, they made a magnificent sight and turned heads as they passed.

As they adjusted their saddles, Tasker said, "That is a fine horse, my friend. What name will you give her?"

Cobb sat proudly, patting the mare's neck. "A horse like this deserves a special name. Sammy Wolf-Killer once signed me of a fearsome Apache chief who called his horse 'Two-Socks.' I will name her 'Missy Two-Socks.'"

A fine name. I've been thinking. We won't be too far

from Serpent's Creek, where we're headed. Maybe after Socorro, we'll stop by and see what's going on.

Cobb nodded, thinking, *I know he wants to see Sammy, the son he never had.*

They bought a decent mule named 'Roscoe' and a sawbuck saddle with pack pads to protect the mule. They would use panniers, large canvas bags fastened to either side of the animal, to carry essentials for several days on the trail.

"Pinkerton did say all expenses paid, didn't he?" Tasker asked sarcastically.

"He did."

The 'essentials' for the detectives included a sturdy axe for chopping wood and building shelter if needed; extra shirts and other clothing; matches; extra ammunition; Arbuckle's Ariosa Blend Coffee, favored by both men; flour; cornmeal; sugar; sorghum molasses; salt; bacon; jerky; hardtack; beans; more beans; an iron skillet; a coffee pot; and basic eating utensils. All these items were to be packed into the panniers, with their weight evenly distributed on each side of the mule. The panniers would then be secured with cinch lines and ropes to keep them stable on rough terrain.

Tasker and Cobb routinely carried various firearms, sometimes requiring different types of ammunition. Since they were traveling cross-country on horseback, it was wise to have firearms of the same caliber to reduce extra ammunition. Tasker carried two 45 Colt Peacemaker revolvers and a specially made .45 Colt 1873 Winchester, while Cobb preferred a .44 Schofield revolver and his cherished 12-gauge cut-down 'coach gun.' The solution was found at the Pinkerton office's extensive armory, where Cobb selected an engraved .45 Colt Peacemaker and turned in his Schofield. The shotgun was not a concern. Both Tasker and Cobb believed it important to have one with them. Therefore, the only extra ammunition needed was .45 Colt and 12-gauge.

These old cavalrymen were no strangers to roughing it on the trail. In cavalry fashion, they used their saddles, rainproof slickers, and saddle blankets to bed down for the night. The saddle or saddlebags could serve as a crude pillow, the slicker as a ground cloth or rain protector, and the saddle blanket would keep them warm on chilly nights. During the day, the saddle blanket went between the saddle and the horse, and the slicker was rolled up and fastened behind the saddle. Horse-shoeing and grooming tools were kept in their saddlebags, along with another box of ammunition, a tin cup for coffee or water, and any odd incidentals needed for immediate use on the trail.

Everything was ready at the livery for an early departure. They brushed down the horses and the mule, then left them alone for a good night's sleep.

Chapter 4

On the Trail

Tasker and Cobb woke at six, shared a hearty breakfast, and arrived at the livery by seven. To ensure their full canteens were secure, they strapped them to the horns of their saddles and added two water skins to the pack mule's load. Sorting Roscoe and saddling their horses took only an hour, and they hit the road south toward Socorro by eight o'clock.

It was a bright, dazzling day. The sun shone down, but the air was dry, and a cool breeze made the journey comfortable. The horses seemed to enjoy the trail work.

"I could get used to this," Cobb said. "Easy ride. We keep an eye on the Rio Grande and the railroad tracks to the south." They followed the old Camino Real de Tierra Adentro, or Royal Road, along the Rio Grande, with intermittent mountains on both sides of the river valley.

"It's been a while since we've ridden the horses for more than a couple of hours. It'll be good for them."

"It will."

On the first night, they camped in a grove of cottonwood trees near a small stream that branched off from the big river not far away. Tasker built a small fire. "I don't reckon a fire will hurt. Haven't heard of any Apache activity in many months."

"They've settled down," Cobb said. He was a good cook, preparing beans, bacon, and corn dodgers over the fire. They bedded down near their hobbled horses.

"I reckon we made about 20 or 25 miles," Tasker said, leaning back on his saddle and gazing at the stars.

Cobb filled a curved pipe, lit it, and took a long pull. "I'd say so. Yes, I could very well get used to this."

They had leftover bacon and corn dodgers for breakfast the next morning and soon set out. They walked at a relaxed pace. Blaze and Two-Socks enjoyed the sunshine, a gentle but welcome breeze, and the sense of freedom on the trail.

Cobb said, "I've been thinking about Abigail."

"We'll find her."

"No, not that Abigail."

"You mean your Abigail Hollis?"

Cobb nodded. "You think...I mean, do you think we could have made it?"

"You and Abigail?"

"Yeah."

"There was a lot of love there." Tasker chuckled. "Even a blind squirrel could see that."

"I mean, maybe love isn't enough. I mean... two different worlds, miles apart."

"You mean Black former slave and White beauty?"

"Harsh, Caleb, but yes, that's exactly what I mean."

"You want my opinion, do you?"

"Your honest opinion."

"Hell, you gotta stop dwelling on that, Jefferson. Alright, here goes. I grew up different, but my time in the 10th Cav made me realize what a real 'man' is – and it sure as hell had nothing to do with his background or the color of his skin.

You're one of the best men I know, and from what I know of Abigail, she was a damned fine woman. Nothing else to say. It would have been rough at times, but if anybody could have made it work, you two would be my first and best bet."

"Kind words, Caleb. Guess I think so, too."

"If she were here, Jefferson, she'd best not catch you having these doubts. She'd likely beat the tar outta you."

They both laughed. "Likely she would, Caleb, likely she would."

"She was some woman," Tasker said.

"Yep." Cobb said nothing for a long while, thinking of making love to Abigail in her father's hayloft. Thinking of the good times – ignoring her untimely death.

After a few hours on the trail, their leisurely ride was interrupted when they spotted a small covered wagon up ahead, pulled by two oxen. The wagon dragged a cow, and a lone rider trotted behind it. He appeared to be a seedy-looking man in a battered derby with an Indian-beaded hatband. He seemed more focused on the dust swirling behind him than on the trail ahead. As they got closer, they noticed another man and a woman driving the wagon. A teenage boy with long blond hair poked his head out between the couple.

"Settlers," Cobb said.

"Farmers, maybe. So who's the saddle tramp riding behind them?"

"Shall we say howdy?"

"Think we should. Polite thing."

They rode up alongside the wagon. As they passed, they got a clearer view of the man riding behind. He was unshaven, with a scraggly, thick mustache and shabby clothes. He also seemed familiar to both detectives, and they exchanged a discreet nod.

"Howdy, what brings you good folks out this way?"

Tasker asked, pulling his horse in close to the wagon. The Pinkerton badges were hidden within their coats.

"Wife, our son, and I are heading for our new homestead down near a place called Socorro," the man said, his long black beard and ready smile on display. His rather plump wife smiled as well. The boy had ducked back into the wagon, which looked full to bursting with household goods.

"Mister Montrose, back there, is leading us, at least to Socorro." The rider in the rear was hanging well back.

"He sold us the homestead," the woman said with pride. "We can hardly wait to get there. It's our dream, ain't it, Bradley?"

"Sure is, mother. A hundred acres with a stream running right through it. Say, where y'all headed?"

Tasker said, "Same general way, to Socorro, at least."

"Well, now. We'd be obliged if you'd join us on the trail. We've been afraid o' them 'paches. Mister Montrose says they're all about these parts and could strike us at any moment if we're not careful."

"He said that, did he?" Tasker looked at Cobb, who raised an eyebrow.

"Tell me about your homestead, Bradley, is it?" Tasker asked.

Bradley and his wife then told the Pinkertons a familiar story. They bought land from Montrose at a high price, trusting his promises of fertile soil and a bright future.

"Mind if I take a look at your deed? I'm fairly familiar with the area around Socorro," Tasker asked.

"I'm so rude," the wife said. "My name's Hester, and my husband here is Bradley, and our boy is Conrad. We're the Larsons." She fumbled through a giant carpetbag as she spoke, finally pulling out some papers.

"Here they are." She handed them to Tasker. "I'm sure

there's nothing wrong. Mr. Montrose handled everything."

Tasker and Cobb examined the documents. It looked like a legitimate deed, with the proper stamps and signatures, and it included a land office map. The map showed the homestead, covering 100 acres, located several miles west of Socorro. Both Tasker and Cobb knew this spot was a barren desert with no water for many miles.

Cobb asked, "Pardon, sir, but would you mind telling us what you paid for this land?"

Bradley Larson was growing increasingly curious and suspicious. "Why," Bradley asked, "what's the problem...and who exactly are you?"

Tasker pulled his coat back, revealing his badge. "We're kind of the law around here. We want to make sure everything is in order."

By this time, the rider had pulled up to the wagon and was listening carefully. He also noticed the badge. Cobb slowly backed his horse, putting him slightly behind the man.

Tasker said, "You don't have to tell me, Mr. Larson, but I'd be obliged."

"Sure, we paid Mr. Montrose five hundred dollars. We was assured by him and his friends that it was a real good deal.

"Hey," Montrose shouted. "You accusin' me of somethin'?"

Tasker ignored him and looked at Bradley Larson. "Mr. Larson, land around this territory sells for about a dollar twenty-five per acre. A hundred acres is roughly a hundred twenty-five dollars, not five hundred. The homestead you bought is in the desert, where there's no water for miles in any direction."

Montrose sneered, "He's a lyin' bastard. Who the hell are you, anyway? The law? Show me a badge."

"We're Pinkertons, Montrose, and that's not your name,

is it?"

"Then yer not the law – not the real law. Yer just Pinks. What the hell you mean that's not my name? Course it is."

By this time, the Larson couple and their boy had gotten off the wagon and were standing in front of it, their eyes wide. Tasker moved his horse between the Larsons and Montrose.

Cobb moved closer to Montrose's horse and pressed his shotgun into the man's back. "Your name's Luke Benteen. We've seen dodgers with a reward on your head all across New Mexico and into Texas. You're a former Comanchero, by God. If that's not enough, you're wanted for armed robbery and murder. The posters look like you, right down to the derby hat with the fancy hatband and that big, fat mustache. You must have posed for them."

"You bastards got no call to hassle me. I ain't done nothin'. That deed's righteous. Now you fellas git, 'fore I get mad."

Cobb laughed, then pressed the shotgun against him harder, pushing Benteen forward in his saddle.

Tasker said, drawing his revolver, "We're takin' you in, Benteen, and we'll collect the reward. Socorro's less than a day's ride. Keep your hands where I can see 'em, and get down off that horse – slowly."

Cobb dismounted at the same time and roughly searched him. He found an old Dragoon pistol tucked into his waistband and a knife on his belt. There was also a Springfield Trapdoor Carbine in a scabbard on his horse. Cobb pulled a wad of bills from Benteen's vest pocket and handed it to Tasker.

"I'd say at least a couple of hundred," Tasker said.

"Wait a minute," Bradley said. "If he's not who he claimed to be, what about us?"

"What about our land?" Hester Larson asked, her voice quivering.

The boy, Conrad, who had disappeared, reappeared behind the wagon with a long double-barreled shotgun that was nearly as big as he was. He aimed it at Benteen. "I'll kill him!" he shouted.

"Easy, lad," Tasker said. "Not this way." He stepped between the boy and Benteen.

Meanwhile, Benteen tried to hide behind his horse. "No! You can't let him kill me!" he shouted.

"I should," Tasker said, "but I won't."

The boy was crying. Cobb moved swiftly and took the gun from him. "Let the law handle him," he said.

Tasker examined the deed again and turned to the Larsons. "I'm afraid you still own the land, worthless or not; it appears legal." He handed the wad of money to Mrs. Larson. "He was greedy, but at least he had some of your money unspent. This is yours. The money was in his pocket. It might compensate you some for your loss. You could try the land."

"No, we won't do that. That dream's been crushed like a bug."

The young boy said, "No homestead. What do we do now, Pa?"

Tasker looked at him. "This is harsh country, lad. I reckon you and your family should head back the way you came. Back to Albuquerque, and start fresh."

"What about the Indians?" Mrs. Larson asked. "This terrible man was our protector."

"Mrs. Larson," Cobb said, "He couldn't protect his own shadow. His pistol's so rusty it's likely to blow up in his face. Besides, there haven't been any Indian troubles around here for a long time."

Tasker and Cobb headed south, with Benteen tied to Tasker's horse on a lead line. They left the Larsons to make their own decisions.

The horses moved at a slow trot. “Pity,” Tasker said.

“It is,” Cobb replied.

Tasker looked back at the Larsons’ wagon heading north. Then he turned back to Cobb as he increased their pace.

“Keep an eye out for a place to bed down,” he said.

Chapter 5

Socorro

If two thousand folks live in Socorro, as the sign says, Tasker thought, *they must be living in cellars. It's three in the afternoon, and this place looks almost deserted.*

The town seemed empty except for the occasional dust swirl or a meandering tumbleweed. They traveled along the main street but saw no sheriff's or marshal's office. An old man sat on the porch of the Grand Hotel, feet propped on the railing, chair leaning back, hat pulled down over his eyes.

"Where is everybody?" Tasker asked.

"Too hot," the man said, not moving from under the wide-brimmed hat. "Folks don't come out much durin' the day 'round here. Sides, it's siesta time, and most folks hereabouts are Mex."

"Lookin' for the law around here."

"No law." This time, the man lifted his hat to glance at the man on horseback, tied between the two Pinkertons. He repeated, "No law."

"No sheriff, no town marshal. Who keeps the peace around here?" Tasker asked.

"Reckon we don't need none. Got us a Vigilance Committee."

Tasker understood exactly what these vigilante-style committees were. Usually, a gang of local citizens decided what the law was on a case-by-case basis and enforced their own sense of justice. "Where might the nearest sheriff or marshal be?"

"I reckon that'd be Fort Craig, a day's ride south. Fort's closed down, but there's still a small detachment o' soldiers. There's word of some kinda judge living in Valverde."

Tasker thought, *Hell, we have business here. We're not traipsing down to this Fort Craig with Benteen.* He asked the old man one more question, "You know a man named Marv Denton hereabouts?"

"Sure, I do. He's one of them fellas on the Vigilance Committee."

"This gets better and better," Tasker said to Cobb.

"It does." Tasker lowered his voice. "We could probably leave Benteen with this committee, but we wouldn't get the reward. Five hundred, as I remember. It's two days down and back to Fort Craig, and no tellin' what we'll find there."

Cobb nodded. "Listen. I have an idea that might fix that problem. How 'bout we find that pig farm first?"

"Excuse me again, sir," Cobb said. "Could you point us toward a large pig farm west of town?"

"You must mean the old Cane pig farm. The owner got himself killed a while back."

"That's the one."

"Straight out the only road west, about five miles. Can't miss it—only thing out that way 'ceptin' sand and scrub. You ain't gonna find anythin' out there but a bunch o' feral hogs. Been deserted fer ages, and them hogs run around free as a bird, eatin' everything in sight. Been nothin' there but them pigs since Cane, the owner, was buried."

"Thanks, mister," Cobb said to the old man.

"Say, where can I find someone on this committee?" Tasker asked.

"At the 'Old Ironsides Saloon,' jus' down the street, this time o' day. Denton will, like as not, be there. He partly owns the place."

Cobb headed toward the small railway station across the street, with Benteen following. Tasker trailed behind, saying, "I see what you're thinking, Jefferson. Good idea."

They located the telegraph room at the station, where a telegrapher was on duty. They summoned a Pinkerton agent to come and pick up Benteen in Socorro as soon as possible. About thirty minutes later, a response arrived stating that an agent was available in Albuquerque and en route. He would meet Tasker and Cobb on the evening train. His orders were to return Benteen to Albuquerque and deliver him to the US Marshal's office there.

"We've got time to scout out this pig farm before he gets here," Cobb said.

"That we do, but let's look up this Denton fella first."

"I can see the saloon from here, Caleb. Let's do it."

Tasker went into the saloon alone, leaving Cobb to watch Benteen. It was a typical, smoke-filled, one-room saloon that reeked of whiskey, beer, sweat, and a hundred other unidentifiable odors. It was dark and gloomy, with no windows and kerosene lamps providing the only light. One man sat at the bar, and there didn't seem to be a bartender.

Tasker said, "Looking for Marv Denton." He walked right up to the man's face.

"Why?" the man asked.

"Maybe I owe him money."

The man stared intently at Tasker. "Do I know you?

What money?"

"So, you're Marv Denton. You don't know me, and I don't owe you money. I wanted to talk to you about a child you brought to the pig farm outside town some time ago." Denton looked suspicious. He was big and ugly, with an almost bald head and one cauliflower ear, a boxer's telltale sign.

"I don't know nothin' about that," Denton said, guarding his words. "Who are you anyway?" When Denton looked at Tasker, he saw a man of average height and build, a contrast to Denton's bulk and over-six-foot frame. He also saw the butt of a Colt Peacemaker showing from under Tasker's coat on the left and the silhouette of a second gun under the coat on the right. He wore a flat hat, cavalry officer-style boots, and spectacles. The glasses made Tasker look a bit bookish. Denton figured him as *no match – easy pickings, in spite of the two guns*.

"How about you answer some questions, Marv?"

"How about you go to hell, mister? I don't gotta answer any questions. Besides, I don't know nothin' about no little boy or no pig farm."

Fast as a rattlesnake, Tasker struck the big man hard in the stomach with his right fist. As Denton collapsed forward, surprised by the force of the blow, Tasker delivered an uppercut to Denton's chin with his left fist. Denton fell back onto the bar. Tasker quickly followed with two blows to Denton's head. Then he grabbed Denton by the vest and shirt with both hands to bring him to his feet.

Tasker growled, "I don't know you, Marv, but I don't like you already. I never said it was a little boy; I said only a child. So tell me, Marv. Tell me about this little boy and the pig farm."

"Back off, mister!" The bartender finally stepped out

from behind the bar, wearing an apron. He was pointing a long, single-barreled shotgun at Tasker. There was an exceedingly loud click as he cocked the hammer.

Tasker froze. Denton pushed away from the bar and wrenched himself free of Tasker's grip. As soon as he was free, he ran out the back door of the bar.

Tasker's town coat had been thrown open. The bartender said, "I see you got a badge. You a marshal or somethin'?"

"Pinkerton," said Tasker.

"You need to get the hell outta here, Mister Pinkerton," the barman said. "We don't like yer kind in these parts."

"OK, I'm going," Tasker said, spreading his hands in front of him, "but I'll be back."

He went outside and mounted his horse. Both his hands were bruised from the fight. Cobb asked, "What happened to your hands?"

"I found Denton, but he ran off. No one else was there except a very unhelpful bartender."

"Your hands?"

"Let's say Denton insisted on attacking me."

Cobb laughed.

Even Benteen chuckled. Cobb snapped, "Shut your mouth!"

Cobb looked at Tasker. "What's next?"

"Let's go for a ride to that pig farm. By the time we get back, our agent should be here."

Chapter 6

The Pig Farm

The farm was so wild and neglected that the Pinkertons nearly missed it. The single-story adobe house was bleak and overgrown. The barn was falling apart, its roof having caved in. It was Benteen who noticed one or two hogs rooting around. They were large, ugly, and black, with coarse hair crusted with dirt, and their tusks were long and fierce.

"Like Micky described it, only worse," Cobb said. "Those hogs could scare the bejesus out of a wild Apache. Think I'll be more careful in the future when I call my new shootin' iron a 'hogleg.'"

He yanked Benteen off his horse and cuffed him to an old wagon lying on its side, missing a wheel. "Don't go anywhere now, Benteen. My Colt is faster than you can run."

"Go to hell," Benteen spat, futilely tugging at the iron handcuffs.

Cobb said, "I will, no doubt, one day."

Tasker and Cobb wandered around the farm, trying to picture Micky tending the pigs and Cane beating him.

"Makes me want to find Abigail even more," Cobb said.

"It does."

They were rounding a corner of the old barn when the shot rang out. A chunk of the barn above Tasker's head chipped away, and he hit the ground. Beside him, Cobb was pointing his Colt in a semicircle toward the spot where the shot had come from.

Tasker whispered, "I'll circle around the barn. You keep him busy."

A second shot rang out, hitting the barn closer to where Cobb lay, but Tasker was already out of sight. Cobb fired three rounds at the spot, then immediately reloaded. He usually carried five rounds with an empty chamber under the hammer for safety, but now he reloaded every chamber.

A third shot hit the grass in front of Cobb's face. He fired two rounds back and heard a thump and a cry of pain. Cobb waited patiently. About a minute later, a burst of gunfire erupted, then everything went eerily silent.

"Got 'im," Tasker called. "Come ahead."

Cobb stood up and walked about thirty yards to where Tasker stood among a patch of piñon trees and tall sycamores.

Tasker said, "Meet Marv Denton. Marv, meet Jefferson Cobb." Denton leaned against an aspen tree, his left arm hanging loosely from a shoulder wound. His right hand was pressed tightly to his side to stop the blood from gushing from a large hole.

As Cobb approached, Tasker said, "Marv, here, has had no luck at all. He took off from the saloon in town and must have come straight here, looking to get the bulge on us."

"Yeah, but Marv's pretty lousy with that Winchester."

"He is."

"What'll we do with him? Leave him for the buzzards?"

"Good idea, Cobb," Tasker said.

Denton finally spoke, breathless. "Ya can't leave me

here. I need a doc. Yer the law, ain't ya?"

"Not exactly," Cobb said. "We're Pinkertons, you know ... civilians. So I reckon we can do just about anything we want with you. Besides, who would know all the way out here?"

"Reckon they'd maybe find your body in a year or two, all bleached bones by then," Tasker said.

"Unidentifiable," Cobb added.

"Or maybe no bones at all." Nearby, a lazy snort sounded, and two scruffy hogs emerged from the brush.

"Jesus, keep them critters away. It hurts, dammit. It hurts real bad. Ya gotta help me."

"Might could do," Cobb said. "Might could do. It'd cost ya, though."

Denton groaned. "What...What is it ya want? Anythin'. Jus' get me to a doctor."

Tasker said, "Those hogs look hungry. I understand they eat everything, even the bones."

Cobb asked, "Why don't you tell us about Cane and this pig farm?"

Denton curled up, trying to make himself as small as possible. He watched the hogs intently. "Nothin' much ta tell. He was a real bastard, hurtin' that boy all the time. I tried ta help him."

"That's bullshit, you scum-suckin' swine. We've talked to the boy," Tasker said, turning to Cobb. "Come on. Let's get outta here. This jasper's already starting to smell."

"When the rot sets in, there's no stopping it," Cobb added. "I understand pigs love the smell of rotting flesh. It perks their appetite."

"No. No. Jus' hold on now. Jus' hold on," Denton pleaded. "Damn. They'll kill me for this."

"Who?" asked Cobb.

"Them. The bosses. They're bigger than you think."

"It seems to me, Jefferson, that this high-binder has only two options: either 'they' kill him or we do."

"Or leave him for the hogs," Cobb suggested. Tasker and Cobb shook their heads, turned around, and walked away.

"Wait. All right. I'll tell ya. Here's how it works. I get a telegram, see, from a man in the East. It tells me one of three things: there's a body coming for disposal here at the pig farm, there's a young boy coming for sale to a client for slave labor or whatever, or there's a young girl coming to be turned out as a whore. The pigs eat the body, and that's done with. The telegram tells us who's buying the young boys, and we take them there. Same with the girls. They tell us where to take 'em, usually a saloon somewhere in New Mexico Territory or Texas, and we do it."

"Where do these bodies for disposal come from, and I don't mean just Chicago or New York City," Cobb asked.

"Hell, I don't know. We guessed the bosses in those two cities are hooked up with other outlaw gangs that kill people and need the bodies disposed of secretly and far, far away from where they were killed."

"Who is the 'we' you spoke of on this end?" Tasker asked.

"You mean in Socorro?"

"That's what I mean."

"It's me … and the whole Vigilance Committee. That's who. That's why I'm a dead man fer tellin' ya all this."

"How do you and the rest get paid?" Cobb asked.

"There's a bank account at First Trust Bank in Socorro. A deposit is made after each assignment is completed. Then, the head of the Committee gives us our share."

"And his name would be?"

Denton lowered his head. "He's my father, Ward Denton,"

he said.

"Who else is on this committee?" Tasker asked, still taking notes.

"Six in total. There's me, my father, my two brothers, Jamie and Tom, George Hanson—the bartender you met at the Old Ironsides Saloon—and the mayor, Samuel Gutiérrez. If needed, we can gather a posse from the townspeople... but they never know what's really goin' on."

"Here's the big question, Marv," Tasker said. "Who sends you the orders and pays the money?"

"A woman in Chicago named Grimm, Mrs. Zelda Grimm. That's all I know. Jus' the name. We get bank checks signed by her."

"New York?"

"I only know the last name, Turpin. That's how the telegrams were signed."

"Tell me about the boy, Micky."

"All I know is that Cane complained the bodies were too much work. They sent him to help."

"And his sister?"

"I don't know nothin'. Maybe El Paso. Many girls were sent there. I took a couple down myself, but that was a long time ago – maybe three years. They were both black, like yer friend here."

Cobb ignored the reference. He was used to ignorant white men. He asked, "So, this committee, where are they sending the boys and girls now? Who's getting rid of the bodies, and where?"

"When Cane was killed, we got scared. The Committee told those in the East they were closing shop. No more kids and no more bodies. Those back East seemed fine with that. My guess is they jus' started up somewhere else, or maybe they already had several places and we was jus' one of them.

I don't know. I don't know. Honest. I jus' don't know anything more. Now, can ya get me to a doc?"

"Not quite," Cobb said. "You said El Paso. Where and to whom did you take these girls there?"

"Shitfire, I don't remember."

"Remember!"

"Ahh. It was to a man named Simms. That's all I know, but I do remember the saloon. It had an odd name — the Fashion Saloon. No idea why. Wait...I remember Simms' first name. It was Oscar. Yup, sure enough, Oscar Simms."

Tasker asked, "What are the committee folks doing about money now?"

"What they've always done before them Eastern folks came along. Occasional hold-ups and collecting money from folks for a hundred miles around. They threaten 'em if they don't pay regular like. They call it 'taxes.'"

Denton was groaning, and blood was pooling beneath him. "That shoulder wound isn't much," Cobb said, "but that stomach wound is bad, real bad."

"Then get me to a doc." He started coughing up blood and collapsed sideways onto the ground.

Tasker and Cobb exchanged glances. They turned and headed back toward their horses, where Benteen was shackled. Tasker, recalling Micky's words, said over his shoulder, "Yeah ... About that, if you make it the five miles back to Socorro, I reckon there'll be a doctor there."

"You bastards!" he gurgled, blood pouring out. "You... you can't do this. This ain't right."

The last thing Tasker and Cobb heard was a series of snorts.

Cobb said, "He wouldn't have made it."

"No. I 'spect not."

They gathered up Benteen and rode back toward Socorro.

Benteen asked, "What the hell went on back there? I heard shots. Thought to myself, what would happen if you two got kilt, me all trussed up like a damn Christmas turkey."

"Good to know you missed us," Cobb said.

Tasker added, "You shouldn't have worried. We were only feeding the pigs."

Chapter 7

Return to Serpent's Creek

"Not much we can do about the Vigilance Committee," Cobb said.

"No," Tasker said. "I feel like a legless dog covered in fleas, but I can't scratch myself."

"Did you just think that up?" Cobb asked, smiling.

"No, but I'd sure feel scratched if I could put that whole bunch behind bars."

"Me too."

"We'll include their names, their practices for disposing of bodies, and all that about robbing and fleecing folks in our report. Let the higher-ups handle them as they see fit."

"We can at least recommend they pass it on to the US Marshals for the territory."

"We can," Tasker said. "I wish old Marshal Sweet were around. He'd let those committee owl hoots have it with both barrels and never blink an eye."

Cobb chuckled.

"Who's this Marshal Sweet?" Benteen asked.

"Shut yer trap, you tiresome little bug!" Cobb snapped. "He was a friend and a lawman. You're not good enough to be a boil on his butt – sure not good enough to mention his name."

Tasker added, "Someone like him won't come around in this world again."

Cobb nodded.

They headed to the Socorro train station, where the Pinkerton agent was waiting for them. "Been here long?" Tasker asked.

"Not long. My name's Holder, Chuck Holder. Is this the big bad Comanchero?"

"It is," Tasker said, shaking Holder's hand. He could feel the strength in the agent's grip. He looked more than capable of handling this pissant.

Cobb also shook Holder's hand and said, "Howdy."

Holder appeared ready to take control. "My orders are to take him off your hands and turn him over to the Marshals in Albuquerque."

As the agent spoke, he took charge of Benteen and put his own handcuffs on him.

"Hey, that hurts," Benteen whimpered.

The agent was a head taller than Benteen and probably twice as heavy. He ignored the outlaw's complaint, grabbing him by the back of his shirt collar, lifting him off the ground. Holder reached into his own vest pocket with his other hand and pulled out a folded piece of paper. "Cartwright says hello. Gave me this to give you."

Tasker pocketed the note without reading it. "Tell him hello back," he said.

"Say, you must be onto something big. They're pretty excited back at headquarters."

Tasker did not respond to the agent's comment but said, "Thanks for coming so quickly."

The train to Albuquerque pulled in, making only a brief stop in Socorro. Holder moved like a cat for someone his size, practically tossing his prisoner onto the passenger car's platform before following him. He smiled at Tasker and Cobb as the train pulled away, and they both nodded in return. Benteen, sprawled on the coach car's platform, raised his cuffed hands and gave a sullen wave.

After the train left, Tasker unfolded the note from Buford Cartwright. It read:

Only a few hints so far. It appears to be a group with potentially malicious intent, possibly operating from New York or Chicago. They pose as the New York Children's Aid Society and claim to be connected to legitimate Orphan Trains – but they are not. Their activities include prostitution, slave labor, extortion, even the occasional murder, and likely several other criminal dealings. The only solid connection so far west is in El Paso, on the Texas border across from Ciudad Juárez, Mexico. Be careful. It's not a safe place for Gringos. Nothing new on Abigail yet. Keep me updated on your progress. May your journeys be winding, risky, and lead to an incredible outcome. Keep your heads down, my friends.

– Buford

"Guess Denton was pretty much telling the truth," Cobb said after reading Buford's findings.

"Yeah, and for a change, we've got even more than Buford. We've got names and a saloon."

"We do."

The Pinkertons left Socorro minutes later, heading south

along the Rio Grande basin. They rode through what remained of Fort Craig and the scattered clusters of businesses and homesteads they called Valverde. It didn't really look like a town. By evening, they reached Serpent's Creek. It had the same official building, the same shops and businesses along north-south Main Street, perhaps a few more saloons, and the same church at the south end of town.

They headed straight to Doc Abbott's house on Custer Street, an adobe-style home surrounded by a white picket fence. The doctor sat in his usual spot on the porch, sipping what was probably his sixth cup of coffee mixed with whiskey. He hadn't changed—gray hair sticking out from under a well-worn straw hat, vest, town coat, and collarless shirt buttoned at the neck. He was tidy as a pin, except for the hat. The wooden crutch he was compelled to use leaned against the wall beside his chair.

"Look what the cat dragged in," he said as they dismounted. "By God, Sammy will be as happy as a clam at high tide to see you two. Maybe not so much, Savannah. She'll think you came to take the lad away."

"Well, that'll be his decision, not our intent, Doc," Tasker said. "How's the wife?"

"Catherine's doin' just fine. Keeps me fat an' sassy. She's inside cookin'. You'll stay for a good home-cooked meal, I reckon." It was a statement, not a question.

"That we will," Cobb said.

Tasker asked, with a note of sarcasm, "Is Mister Wolf, the former Wolf-Killer, around?"

Sammy signed, *"Here!"* clapping his hands as he rounded the corner of the house, a big grin on his face, *"but you can call me 'Samuel."*

"I'll call you 'Snip,' and you'll like it," Cobb signed back and said at the same time, grinning. Snip had always been

Cobb's pet name for Sammy, except when he was upset with him.

Sammy ran up to Cobb and gave him a hug. Then he wrapped his arms around Tasker, who bristled but eventually relented.

"Sammy Wolf," Tasker said. "It suits better than Wolf-Killer for an up-and-coming lad like yourself."

They walked into the house. Doc said, "I'll be in shortly."

"How have you been, Snip?" Cobb asked after they sat down at the kitchen table.

"Happy, but bored stiff," Wolf signed.

"Savannah?" Tasker asked, touching his arm to get his attention.

"She's fine. Amazing." He signed, leaning forward. *"She's a keeper, Caleb. I think I love her."*

"I'm shocked," Tasker said mockingly.

"Me too," Cobb chimed in.

"So, when's the big day?" Tasker asked.

Sammy replied, *"Marriage? I don't know. Do we have a new assignment?"*

"We have a new assignment, Sammy, but what about you? I don't know. You look pretty happy. Maybe it's time for you and Savannah to settle down. Besides, we heard you're the law around here now."

"Yes. They appointed me town marshal a while back, but it's quiet as a grave hereabouts. Occasionally, a drunk, someone roughing up his wife, or a petty thief. Small stuff. I sure miss the trail. Wind in His Hair hasn't had a good run since you two left. Anyway, don't count me out."

"What about your marshal duties? You'd just pack up and leave the townsfolk in mortal danger," Tasker asked.

"I have a deputy who can do the job just fine if I'm away. We're a team, he and I – always together. His mother taught

him sign language because his sister couldn't speak. My rapid-fire lip-reading comes in mighty handy, and he basically talks for me when I'm town marshaling."

Sammy paused, looked from Caleb to Jefferson, then slowly signed, *"We're still a team, aren't we?"*

"You know we are, Snip," Cobb said. He knew Sammy could read lips as fast as most people could spew out their thoughts, but he spoke slowly, looking into Sammy's eyes to emphasize his words. "Too much trail dust under our feet to be anything else. What Caleb's saying is that you have a life here. A good life, and a fine woman. Maybe it's time for you to settle down. Might be the only chance you get."

"Look at us," Tasker cut in. "Free and easy is fine, but it doesn't keep your feet warm on a cold night." Tasker remembered Sarah, the woman he had loved more than life, shot by an outlaw and thrown from a moving train.

"In my experience," Tasker continued, "that thing we call love, which you've got right here and right now, doesn't come around that often." Both Wolf and Cobb knew Tasker was remembering Sarah, and Wolf listened carefully. Cobb had his own memories of the lovely Abigail Hollis, daughter of a local storekeeper, willing to spend her life with him, a black man in a white world. She, too, had been killed in this same town not long ago. He grieved and thought of her too many times every day.

"I just don't know," Wolf signed.

"I do." It was Savannah, standing in the kitchen doorway, the same brown-haired beauty Tasker and Cobb remembered. All three men turned toward her, thinking the same thing—*Uh-oh, we're in for it now.*

To their amazement, Savannah said, "I want you to take him with you."

There was a long pause, and its silence was louder than a

train passing on a dark night. Doc Abbott was moving from the porch into the kitchen. Upon hearing Savannah's words, he swung around sharply, nearly falling over his crutch, and went back to the porch.

Savannah said, speaking to all three men at the table. "Don't you men know anything? You think I'm stupid? I can't see what's right in front of me? Gracious, I don't believe you men. I know Samuel loves me. I also know he's restless and bored, and it's driving him crazy. It's not because of me. It's his nature. I've tried to smooth out some of the edges, asking him to change his name and all, but it doesn't work. I now realize it was all wrong. You can't cage the man he is. The man I love."

Sammy tried to stop her, signing *"Savannah, you..."*

Savannah stepped into the room and held her arm straight out, palm forward and aimed directly at Sammy. "I really do know you love me, you chucklehead, but the man I chose to love has a wild streak. A wildness born in you that will never go away. You all have it. I accept that. It's part of why I love you, Samuel. If I stifled that passion, you wouldn't be the man I love."

"So here it is," she said, facing Tasker and Cobb. "You take Samuel on whatever adventure you must, but you make damn sure he comes back to me – in one piece. Somewhere in our lives, we'll get married, maybe even have children. Maybe he'll stay with me for a while when that happens; that'll be his choice. But there's one thing I'll never do. I'll never tie him to my skirts and deprive him of the freedom and adventure he craves. I'd hate myself if I did that, and I 'spect he'd come to hate me too. You bring him back to me when you can. I'll be here waiting."

Savannah turned and left the room. Sammy kicked his chair out and followed her.

"Damn," was all Cobb could say.

Tasker said nothing, then blinked.

Catherine stood in the kitchen doorway, saying, "Soup's on."

Neither Sammy nor Savannah said anything else at the table or for the rest of the evening. At dawn the next day, Tasker and Cobb saddled up and prepared to leave. They hadn't seen Savannah or Sammy since supper the day before. They hadn't pursued the matter of Sammy coming along, both thinking it had to be Sammy's decision.

"Guess I'll see you boys next time around," Doc Abbott said. He was still sitting in the same chair on the porch.

"Reckon so," Tasker said.

"You take care of yourself, Doc, and look out for Sammy and Savannah," Cobb said.

"Sorry if we caused a ruckus," Tasker said.

"I'll take care of 'em. You boys watch yourselves." Doc Abbott nodded, smiled, and lit his long, curved pipe.

They rode out of town past the church and cut over toward the Rio Grande. As they approached a rise about a mile out, they saw a rider waiting by the trail. He was mounted on a roan Mustang with a long, flowing mane.

Cobb shouted, "Sammy!" He and Tasker broke into a quick trot, waving as they approached. The newly named Sammy Wolf waved back.

As the horses gathered and shuffled, no words were spoken, only smiles. After about a minute, the horses had calmed down. Tasker looked at Cobb and Wolf. "Let's ride."

Chapter 8

El Paso

The three Pinkerton men arrived late in El Paso and boarded their horses at a livery stable near the hotel. After days on the trail, they decided that a night of rest in a comfortable bed was in order.

Tasker arranged a room at the Grand Central Hotel with two beds and a cot. He knew Sammy Wolf usually preferred to sleep on the floor, but now, with his new sophistication, he might choose a bed. Either way, the cot was available.

Both Tasker and Cobb had previously visited El Paso while serving in the 10th Cavalry. Like many frontier towns, El Paso grew significantly after the arrival of the major stagecoach line, the Butterfield Overland Stage, followed by the railroad. It became a thriving border town. Its Mexican counterpart across the Rio Grande, El Paso del Norte, was in the process of changing its name to Ciudad Juárez to honor Mexican leader Benito Juárez. On the American side, brick buildings began replacing adobe structures, and a few businesses even installed electric lights.

Tasker knew that Cobb had a brief fling with a local madam named Etta Clark during their 10th Cavalry days.

Clark was a French Canadian who ran one of the few brothels in El Paso that didn't discriminate based on race, allowing Blacks, Whites, Mexicans, and some Indians to use her services and those of her girls. However, she still excluded Chinese laborers. This selective non-discrimination policy was clearly shown by a black-and-white checkerboard border painted along the front of her establishment. She was a small, lovely woman who spoke with a charming French accent.

Etta Clark's main rival, 'Big Alice' Abbott, ran a brothel across the street. She was six feet tall and weighed over two hundred pounds. Both her brothel and Etta's were in the 'Tenderloin district' of El Paso, an area where prostitution and other vice activities flourished with little law enforcement interference.

Back in the privacy of their hotel room, the three detectives discussed strategy. Cobb suggested, "Let's not go directly to the Fashion Saloon and ask for Oscar Simms. I'd like to go see Etta first, reestablish old ties, and check the lay of the land."

"Who's Etta?" Wolf signed.

"An old friend from our cavalry days," Cobb said.

"Back when we were wild young lads, like you," Tasker joked. "But I think you're onto something, Jefferson. First thing tomorrow, but you'd better go alone."

Cobb took a mule-drawn streetcar to the Tenderloin District and found Etta Clark's place on Utah Street. He was stunned when he walked in. Not only did Etta recognize him, but she ran to him and wrapped her arms around his neck. "*Mon dieu, mon grand amant sombre* – my big dark lover. *Depuis combien de temps*? How long has it been?"

Embarrassed, Cobb pulled himself slightly away from her intense grip. "*Trop long*, too long," he managed to blurt out, apologizing for his limited French, "*Vous savez que mon français est limité, oui.*"

"But of course, *mon amoureux*. I will speak to you in American, but your French is excellent. What draws my dark lover back to me? No, never mind. Come with me." She seized his hand with unusual strength for such a small woman and half-dragged him upstairs to her bedroom. The other women, sprawled in the lavish living room, half-dressed, watched in wonder as their stern madam, who never went out with anyone, disappeared up the stairs, Cobb following behind.

At the top of the stairs, she turned and yelled at the girls, "*Mon dieu*! Have you never seen a *guerrier noir* before? I see it in your eyes. You are jealous. Well, you should be. Now get back to business, or I will deduct your laziness from your pay."

Her boudoir was lavish and uninhibited, with silk curtains, ornate and expensive furniture, and a large bed with silk sheets that matched the curtains. Etta Clark complemented the carefree atmosphere of her surroundings. In her early forties, she remained remarkably beautiful. She had a slender figure, high cheekbones, and jet-black, silky hair that fell to her waist when let down, which it soon was.

Cobb didn't return to his hotel until late afternoon.

Tasker and Wolf waited patiently, with Tasker taking notes in his notebook and Wolf carefully cleaning the Vernier peep sight on his prized .45-70 Trapdoor rifle. Wolf could read lips as fast as anyone could speak, so he watched Cobb's face for what would come next.

Cobb distracted them by asking, "So, what have you two been up to today?"

Wolf raised his rifle and signed, *"Cleaning."*

Tasker said, "Learned a couple of things. Stoney Jenkins, a former Texas Ranger, is the current City Marshal of this fine community, which seems to hire and remove its marshals as often as most folks change their socks. I've worked with him before. Good man. We'll talk to him first thing tomorrow. I also found the Fashion Saloon, which wasn't easy. See, most folks hereabouts call it 'The Wigwam.' No idea why. You've been gone half a day. You find anything useful, 'cept the size of Etta Clark's boudoir?"

Wolf burst into loud laughter.

"Matter of fact, I did," Cobb said forcefully. Wolf stifled a laugh.

"Pray tell," Tasker said.

"First of all, this Simms cretin is a piece of horse droppings. Known around El Paso as a sleazy panderer, a pimp with two or three girls. The ladies come and go. It's rumored some disappear. He apparently keeps them living in a wooden-sided wagon, like a snake oil salesman's cart. A pretty big one, all painted up to advertise his 'wares.' He makes a circuit with his wagon about once a month, going as far as the silver and copper mining camps up toward Lordsburg and Silver City. When he's not on the road, his girls work at the Wigwam, and the saloon owner takes a cut."

"Let's hope he's not on the road right now," Tasker said. Wolf nodded in agreement.

"He's not," Cobb said, "according to my very, very reliable source. He got back yesterday."

Tasker and Cobb visited the City Marshal the following morning, while Wolf remained at the hotel. When in a town, he preferred to stay out of the way. Besides, three detectives talking to people could be a bit intimidating.

Marshal Stoney Jenkins was sitting in his office, feet propped on his desk, reading a newspaper. "Stoney, how they hangin' pard?" Tasker said. Jenkins practically jumped out of his chair and grabbed Tasker's hand, shaking it vigorously.

"I'm good, I'm good. Every day above the grass is a fine day. What brings you into my world, old friend?"

"Long story," Tasker said. "By the way, this is Jefferson Cobb, my partner."

"Howdy, Jefferson. Too bad they got you workin' with this jasper."

"Howdy back. It's a challenge at times," Cobb said, amused.

"Say, Caleb, you still with that Pinkerton fella?"

"I am. I'm lookin' for a man named Oscar Simms. You know him?"

"Hell, everybody in El Paso knows Simms," Jenkins sneered, looking at Tasker. "He's one of the 'jack' brothers – either 'off' or 'ass.' A real troublemaker. What's he done now?"

Tasker explained why they were searching for him. "I understand he hangs out at the Fashion Saloon or whatever they're calling it these days."

"I saw him on my rounds last night," Jenkins said, "at the saloon. Most folks are calling it the Wigwam Saloon nowadays, with new owners."

"You know anything about his activities?"

"I know he runs a couple of whores out of that wagon of his. The city would love to get rid of his ass, but he manages to stay just out of the law's reach. I'd sure be open to putting him in jail, but there's no evidence, and his girls won't say a word, too scared, I reckon. He hangs around with some pretty bad hombres."

Cobb asked, "You mind if we take a shot at him?"

"Be my guest, boys, but be careful."

"We don't aim to be too gentle," Cobb said. "Might ruffle some feathers, make your job tougher."

"Don't you worry none about that, Jefferson. This crowd

y'all are after makes me sick. You boys take your best shot. I'll back you."

"Thanks, Stoney," Tasker said. "Just like the old times."

Tasker and Jenkins entered through the front door of the Wigwam Saloon. Cobb and Wolf covered the back. Even in the dark, smoky room, Simms was clearly visible.

"That's him by the piano," Jenkins said.

Simms looked seedy yet dangerous, with a revolver low on his right hip. He spotted Jenkins and bolted out a side door at full speed. Tasker and Jenkins gave chase, but when they exited the saloon, Simms was nowhere in sight. Cobb and Wolf came around the building from behind.

"You see him?" Tasker shouted.

"Not a sign," Cobb said. They headed back into the saloon, where Jenkins was talking with the bartender.

"He wasn't particularly helpful," Jenkins said, "but he did give me the names of Simms's current whores. They weren't in the saloon. Their names are Lucy, Lucinda, and Jasmine. Jasmine's a very pretty quadroon, Lucy's a brown-haired looker, and Lucinda's kinda ugly. My guess is they're in his wagon. It's supposed to be behind the mercantile store two doors down. No idea why he ran, unless he knows you're after him."

"That might be the case," Tasker said. "This gang has long tentacles, reaching all the way east to New York, and we weren't too subtle when questioning people up in Socorro."

They moved to the back of the mercantile, but there was no sign of Simms, the girls, or the wagon. They searched along the street, both in front and behind, but found nothing. After about an hour, they gave up and walked back to the hotel with Jenkins.

"Thanks for your help, Stoney," Tasker said. "I think he's hightailed it with those girls. We'll take it from here. Get after him tomorrow in daylight. We have a third detective with us, and he's an excellent tracker."

"My pleasure, Caleb. You and Jefferson, keep yer heads down. If you need me or any of my contacts, like a few Rangers, you whistle. I mean that."

The next morning, Wolf didn't take long to find the wagon tracks behind the livery. They headed south toward Juárez and Mexico. *"Looks like he crossed the border,"* he signed.

"No matter," Tasker said. "We're going after him."

Cobb said, "I want to make a stop before we leave, Caleb."

"I think I know where," Tasker said, both he and Wolf grinning. "We'll be waiting at the edge of town. Take your time."

Cobb went to see Etta at her place.

She was there, smiling at him. "I wanted to say goodbye and thank you for your help," he said.

"It was nothing, *mon ami*. You know I would do anything for you." She wrapped her arms around Cobb's neck, stood on her toes, and kissed him on the lips, long and passionately. He returned the kiss with equal fervor.

"You are, I think, my only guilty pleasure, mon seul plaisir coupable, in a world full of sadness and turmoil. Come back to me when you can, my lover. I will be waiting, always."

Cobb, warmed by her genuine passion, said, "*Au revoir, ma belle*." He ran his fingers through her hair, paused briefly, then left.

Chapter 9

Ciudad Juárez

It was a blazing sunny day with no breeze. You could see the heat shimmer rising like ripples over the trail ahead.

Cobb said, "You could sizzle steaks on a flat rock in this heat."

"You could," Tasker replied.

"It's only Mexico. It's always like this," Wolf signed.

They had little trouble following the wagon. With three women and Simms, pulled by a four-horse team, it was heavy, and the wheels left clear grooves in the sand road. Crossing into Mexico was easy—they passed an old sign, riddled with at least twenty bullet holes, that had almost erased the message. In English and Spanish, it read: YOU ARE NOW ENTERING MEXICO.

"Juárez up ahead," Wolf signed.

"Doesn't look like much," Tasker observed, "Adobe houses and the one church steeple over what looks like an adobe church."

Wolf rode ahead into town but returned quickly. *"Too many tracks,"* he signed. *"Lost the wagon."*

"Let's try the church first. Ask some questions," Cobb

suggested.

Tasker said, “If that doesn’t work, we’ll ride around the town’s outer ring and hopefully cut a trail.”

“Could be they’re right here in Juárez.”

“More likely, they rode through and kept heading southward.”

The late afternoon sun cast a silvery glow across the old church’s adobe walls as they arrived and tied their horses to a hitching post. The walls stood tall and proud, as if carved by the hand of God himself. The heavy wooden doors stood open, and above them in a niche was the faded statue of a saint. Inside, the church was unexpectedly cool and welcoming, much like the over six-foot-tall, muscular padre, who wore an oversized straw sombrero and black robes.

He greeted them warmly, “Ah, my friends, come in. Yer always welcome in the House of God. I would be askin’ ya to kindly leave those guns on the hooks near the door, this bein’ a place for worship, not for violence.”

“You speak English very well, Father,” Tasker said.

“Not the King’s English, though. I’m Irish, ya see. Father Shamus O’Leary at yer service… guns, please, gents?”

“We’re Pinkertons, Father. We’re searching for a man driving a wagon carrying three ladies.”

“I see,” the Padre said. He reached into his robes and drew out an old but intimidating Colt Walker pistol, which he pointed at the ground in front of him. “I’ve asked ya twice, nicely. Guns? … Please?”

Tasker finally understood. He nodded to Cobb and Wolf. All three removed their gun belts and hung them on the wooden pegs beside the door.

The revolver disappeared into the Padre’s robes. “Now, what about this man with the ladies?”

"He’s not a good man, Father,” Tasker said. “In fact, we

believe the women are with him against their will. He deals in slave labor and prostitution, for starters."

"It doesn't surprise me. He hurt some of my flock while askin' for information. He's about a day's ride ahead of you."

"What information?" Cobb asked.

"About an unused road leadin' out of town. "Wait …" he called out, "José Vargas!" Get yer scrawny backside in here, sharpish!"

A small man, dressed in white and wearing a straw sombrero typical of a peasant farmer, entered the doorway where the padre stood. He was all smiles.

"Good lad," the padre said in a much kinder tone.

"*Sí, padre. ¿Qué necesita?*"

"Tell these kind gentlemen about the man with the *putas* and the big wagon, *en inglés*."

The Padre looked at Tasker and said, "José speaks excellent English."

"*Si, Padre*," he said, turning to the detectives. "They come last night to my home. Beat my brother, Benito, because he doesn't tell them what they want to know."

"What was that?" Tasker asked.

"The man he want us to show him the old military road heading northwest. Benito, he doesn't speak the good English, so the man hit him many times. I come in from the fields, or the man, he might have killed Benito."

"What road is this?"

Father O'Leary interjected, explaining, "That would be the old Spanish road. Starts about a mile south of Juárez. The Conquistadores used it as far back as the sixteenth century. It'll get ya as far as Lordsburg, New Mexico Territory, but no farther. It goes through some mountainous terrain. No doubt that's why the Conquistadores abandoned it."

"Clever bastard, this Simms," Tasker said. "He's doubling back north, thinking we'll push south."

Cobb asked José, "Can you show us this road?"

"*Sí, Senior*, for a price."

They all laughed. "Fair enough," Cobb said. He took out several silver coins and handed them to José.

True to his word, José pointed out where the military road began south of Ciudad Juárez.

"The wagon wheel tracks are even deeper than the ones we followed to Juárez," Wolf signed. *"They must have gathered more supplies. They'll be easy to follow."*

They rode back to the church to thank the Padre for his help. As they prepared to leave, Father O'Leary said, "I was happy to help, gentlemen, but you must go now. Your guns don't belong in our peaceful town."

He took Tasker aside and whispered, "Before you go, a word of warning. Five pistoleros, the slimy kind, not real vaqueros, passed through here earlier today. I strongly suspect they were lookin' fer you. They did not take the military road but continued south. I think you must be careful. Watch yer back, my son, or you and yer friends might come to an early grave."

"Gracias, Father, for your hospitality, your information, and your kind warning. We are in your debt, and we will be careful."

Father O'Leary called from the church as they rode away, "Fair weather and a following wind, me boyos. *Dios esté contigo*."

"What a character," Cobb said once they were out of earshot.

"He is," replied Tasker as they rounded a bend onto a narrow Juárez street.

Wolf, who was in front, quickly pulled Wind to a stop. *"Ahead!"* he signed, but Tasker and Cobb had already seen them and pulled their mounts to a halt.

Facing them were four vaqueros on horseback, fifty yards away. Adobe houses lined both sides of the street they were on.

Tasker yelled to Wolf, "Get up high!"

Wolf knew exactly what Tasker wanted. He had done the same thing many times before to cover Tasker and Cobb from a high point or rooftop. He quickly moved Wind into an alleyway and stood on his saddle to boost himself onto one of the adobe buildings. Meanwhile, Tasker and Cobb, wanting to give Wolf time to get into position, stared down the vaqueros, daring them to shoot. The vaqueros didn't seem eager to open fire or start a gunfight.

Wolf moved parallel to the street toward the vaqueros, one roof at a time. When Tasker and Cobb saw that Wolf was close enough to cover them, they opened fire on the Mexicans. The Mexicans decided it was time and began returning the detective's fire. As soon as they did, Tasker and Cobb, without hesitation or command, charged straight at them.

The vaqueros were stunned and confused by the sudden ferocity of the attack. They began to scatter, but it was too late. Tasker shot the two on the right with two shots from his Colt revolver. Cobb shot the two on the left off their horses with his shotgun, one barrel at a time.

A loud shot rang out, and a fifth vaquero tumbled from a rooftop, his head shattered by a .45-70 round. Wolf peeked his head up from a rooftop across the street, smiling down at the two Pinkertons. There had been a sixth vaquero on the roof where the young half-Apache now stood. As Wolf moved from rooftop to rooftop, he saw the man lying in wait. Wolf came up behind him and stabbed him with his knife. Only then did he take aim at the vaquero on the opposite roof and blow his head off. The entire gunfight lasted less than a minute.

Wolf jumped down from the roof and remounted Wind, who had joined Tasker and Cobb. The three Pinkertons continued riding their horses south out of Juárez as if they hadn't killed six Mexican men. Only Wolf was slightly sweaty from running along the rooftops.

"They really don't want us looking into this," Cobb said, referring to whoever was behind the criminal enterprise.

"They don't," Tasker replied.

Wolf nodded.

CHAPTER 10

THE MILITARY ROAD

When they reached the junction south of town, they turned northwest onto the military road. Wolf was in the lead. He was able to move Wind at a normal walking pace while keeping an eye on the wagon wheel ruts in the road.

After an hour of riding, Cobb suggested, "We've gotta make up a day. We should pick up the pace."

"I figure the wagon will slow down quite a bit when it reaches the mountains," Tasker said. "We should overtake 'em easily. I'd rather keep the horses at a walk."

"Caleb's right," signed Wolf. *"They're likely to slow to a crawl. This wagon we're following is too wide and too heavy for mountain trails. We'll catch up to them soon enough."*

"Ganging up on me, are ya, Snip?" Cobb said, grinning. "I 'spect yer right, though."

As soon as they reached the first foothills, the terrain became rougher for the horses. The trail narrowed and began to wind around rock formations. They reached the top of the first mountain and saw the wagon a mile or so down the trail, leaning forward and to one side.

"Looks like they lost a wheel," Tasker said, "and I only see three horses standing."

They urged their horses into a trot, with Tasker taking the lead. The wagon was at a steep, downward angle as it descended the grade. The horses were still hitched, and one of them, on the front right, lay down under the harnesses, snorting heavily.

Two women sat on the ground to one side, crying. Another woman, the quadroon, sat on a boulder, her face showing clear signs of a beating. All three were shoeless and partially dressed. The two women on the ground had their hands tied behind their backs. Simms was sweating and cursing quietly, trying—unsuccessfully—to lift the front right of the wagon with a small, inadequate wagon jack. He didn't notice or hear the detectives until they rode up behind the wagon and pulled their horses sharply to a stop in front of him.

"What the hell!" he exclaimed, dropping the jack.

"Good day, sir," Tasker said. "Would you mind explaining what's going on here?" He noticed Simm's sidearm, a small .36-caliber pocket gun, lying on the ground nearby, atop his coat.

"You blind or somethin'? I'm changin' a damn wheel! That's what I'm doin'."

"I can see that," Tasker said, "but I also see ladies all tied up, two of them crying."

"They're jus' whores. Don't make no never mind. An' I don't want 'em sneakin' up on me from behind. I value my skull too much."

"So, are we to understand you're keeping these ladies against their will?" Cobb asked.

Simms reached for his pistol, but the sight of Cobb's two cocked shotgun barrels made him change his mind. A few yards away, Wolf dismounted and went to free the two tied women. He moved to the quadroon sitting on the boulder and leaned over to see if she was bound as well. As he did so, she grabbed his knife, pushed him off balance, and rushed at Simms.

In one quick stroke, she slit his throat from ear to ear. Simms grabbed his throat with both hands as blood gushed through his fingers. The other two women were right behind the quadroon, kicking and punching the dying, gasping Simms.

"Shit," Tasker muttered, realizing he wouldn't get any answers about Abigail's whereabouts from a dead man.

The quadroon handed the bloody knife back to Wolf, who had regained his balance and looked sheepish.

She said, "Thanks for the loan. I feel much better now. My name is Jasmine. These two ladies are Lucy and Lucinda. We were all sold to this animal some time back." She pointed toward Simms' body, lying in a growing pool of blood. "He deserved much more than we gave him."

"I 'spect so, ma'am," Tasker said, "but I'm afraid it doesn't help us much." He explained that they were Pinkertons and that they were looking for Abigail, then described her in detail.

Jasmine said, "We... Well, I know her. I remember the scar on her face. She showed me another one on her ankle. It was the number '12,' crudely done, I guess, with a knife. Really creepy."

The detectives' interest was piqued. *This could be our first real lead*, Tasker thought.

Jasmine continued, "She was with Lucy and me for a while before they sold us off."

Tasker asked, "How long ago was that?"

"Maybe two or three months, maybe more," Lucy said.

"Who was she sold to?"

"Never saw anybody. Never got a name, but it was in Lordsburg."

"Well, that's something," Tasker said, "and that's where we're headed. You ladies get dressed. We'll fix this wagon and bury our friend here. Cobb, you and Wolf unhitch the team. Simms didn't know much about repairing a wagon. Then let's unload it. It needs to be much lighter, especially on this grade. After that, we can fix the wagon more easily and put this critter underground."

With the wagon lightened and free of the horse harness, it was easy to rig a makeshift lever system using logs and ropes, lift the wagon, remove the lynchpin, and slide the broken wheel off the axle. The axle was greased, and the spare wheel was installed.

To be safe, Wolf was sent down the back trail to make sure they weren't being followed. He returned with a report that the area was clear for miles. He did the same ahead of the wagon and brought back the same report.

While Wolf was gone, Tasker and Cobb loosened the injured horse from the traces and freed its partner standing nearby. For balance, it was better to keep it a two-horse rig. The downed horse had broken its leg and was in severe pain.

When Wolf returned and saw the suffering animal, he knew what had to be done. He didn't want to risk alerting anyone by shooting, so he did the only thing he could. He put the horse out of its misery by slitting its throat. He did this out of sight of the women.

Later, the women confronted Tasker. "What about us?" Jasmine asked.

Tasker replied, "We'll take you as far as Lordsburg. We'll sell the wagon and horses there, then get you tickets to wherever you want to go, and wish you well. I'm afraid that's the best we can do. We're not out here on a lark. We have a job to do. Frankly, you've made that job harder by killing Simms, not that he didn't deserve it."

Cobb told the ladies, "I'm afraid you'll have to stay out of the wagon when we're moving. There's too much weight being carried across these mountains with only two horses pulling. You can sleep in the wagon at night, of course."

"I'll drive the wagon," Wolf signed to Cobb, who translated to the women. *"One of you can ride the horse that isn't pulling the wagon, and the other can ride my horse, Wind-in-His-Hair. He's gentle and loves women."* When Cobb translated the signing, the ladies smiled. Lucy's smile grew even broader as she shot Wolf a fiery stare. He blushed.

Chapter 11

Through the Mountains

The rest of the journey to Lordsburg went smoothly. The three detectives took turns watching for any unwanted guests. They weren't followed, and as time went on, they came to better appreciate the three women they were protecting.

To the amusement of Cobb and Wolf, the usually stoic Tasker seemed to be quite enchanted by Jasmine, and she by him. They couldn't blame him. She was beautiful, strong, and outspoken to a fault. She was also the indisputable leader among the women, yet she held that position without ever seeming to exert authority.

Jasmine had long auburn hair, captivating blue eyes, smooth, flawless almond skin, and a slender figure. She was about the same height as Tasker but somehow looked taller. On the first night of their mountain trek, she sat next to Tasker by the campfire.

They talked late into the night. She teased him about being a big, tough lawman who wore spectacles and, in her opinion, was way overeducated for his role. He, naturally, bristled a bit, saying he could see her just fine without the glasses. He then joked that West Point had never been accused of overeducating anyone. Finally, they fell asleep lying beside each other.

The following night, as they sat by the fire, Jasmine was adamant that she wasn't going anywhere. She was angry but determined to stay and help find Abigail. "I can help," she argued. "I can identify Abigail and any of the men who put her on the 'line' as a prostitute." It was a claim the Pinkertons had to at least consider.

Lucy shamelessly pursued Wolf, but with Savannah always on his mind, the young man managed to remain chaste and loyal. He consistently remained courteous around the women, especially Lucy.

Cobb had no interest in Lucinda or anyone else, though he was always kind and considerate toward them all. He kept to smoking a well-worn pipe and reading a threadbare copy of Sun Tzu's 'The Art of War', which he kept in his saddlebags. Cobb bore old wounds all over his body from being mistreated as a slave, followed by twenty years in the cavalry and numerous violent encounters alongside Tasker. Despite the constant pain, he never let it show.

On the last night before reaching Lordsburg, they camped on high ground. The night was filled with stars watching over the small group of travelers below. The group could see for miles in every direction, as if the distant specks of light were protecting them. They all settled down early.

It was past midnight, and Tasker couldn't sleep. Jasmine, as she had every night, slept peacefully and safely beside him, both soaking up the warmth of the fire. Tasker stood without disturbing her and walked a little way from the camp. He paused among a scattering of oak and piñon pines to gaze at the guardian stars, recognizing the constellations he had learned at West Point. First, the North Star; then Ursa Major, the great bear; Leo, the majestic lion; and finally, Virgo, the maiden. He felt a hand slip into his. It didn't frighten or even startle him. He knew Wolf was nearby, on guard. Besides, the hand was too soft, too gentle. Jasmine was beside him, also looking upward. She had a blanket wrapped around her slim frame to keep out the night's chill.

Tasker knew she had been used as a prostitute, but he also understood it hadn't been her choice. He had been thinking about it over the last few nights, with her so close. It wasn't a moral dilemma. He was no prude, and he had been with many other women himself. After all, even his lovely Sarah had been a businesswoman, owning a saloon with many women on her payroll. *It's simple*, he thought. *I haven't had much luck with women in my life. Am I afraid to open those gates again?* He didn't like seeing himself as such a frightened fool. As he stood there holding Jasmine's hand, he made a decision. *I don't care about the past, mine or hers. I'm not a coward. Jasmine is a beautiful, smart, desirable woman.*

He took her in his arms. She willingly melted into his embrace. Their lips met. Their kiss spoke to the burning desire they both felt. Jasmine dropped the blanket, placed her hands behind his neck, ran her fingers through his hair, and pulled his face toward hers. Their second kiss was an intense buildup of passionate desire. She drew him down onto the crumpled blanket. They fumbled with their clothing until they were in a nude embrace. The tenderness and intimacy that followed were slow and welcoming. Tasker had never felt the fiery excitement he felt now, not even with Sarah, whom he had loved dearly. Jasmine momentarily forgot the dark times and felt like a young woman again, overwhelmed with pure joy. There was no sleep. They spent the night making love and gazing at the stars.

When they returned to camp the next morning, only Wolf was awake, making coffee. He said nothing, but his grin said it all. After they settled by the fire, Wolf signed, *"Coffee?"*

Chapter 12

Lordsburg

Entering Lordsburg the next day, Tasker gathered the ladies for a talk. "Ladies, Jasmine wants to stay with us for a while to help identify Abigail and any of the lowlifes around. Lucy and Lucinda, you can keep the wagon, whatever's in it, the harness, and the three horses. If you sell them, that should give you enough money to get wherever you want to go."

Lucy spoke up. "We talked. We both want to go home. We'll send telegrams to our folks to see if there's still a place for us. Thank you for all you've done. We'll miss your company, Jasmine. Best of luck."

A series of demonstrative goodbyes followed, leaving the three detectives feeling a bit awkward. This was especially true for Wolf, who was quite flustered by Lucy's long, passionate parting kiss.

When the two women left to go their separate ways, Tasker said, "Sammy, I think you need a cold bath."

"I'll be glad to help," Jasmine said in jest. "Then we can send a telegram to… what's her name… Savannah."

"I'm fine," Sammy said soberly, his face as red as a cherry. "I don't need any help, thank you."

After securing rooms at the Copper Inn — one for Tasker, Cobb, and Wolf, and another for Jasmine — Tasker asked her to discreetly visit the larger saloons in Lordsburg. She was to ask a few questions as if she were looking for a job and to look for Abigail or anyone she might recognize. Tasker visited each place separately to keep her safe. After a long day with little luck, Jasmine recognized someone in the Bloody Bucket.

She sat down with Tasker at a table and said, "I know that dude at the bar. The one with the fancy black boots and the high derby. He has very long hair, but it's tied at the back. That's why I didn't recognize him right away. He's definitely the one who sold me to Simms and one of the men from somewhere back East who brought other girls to the saloons where I worked in El Paso and Ciudad Juárez."

"Did he recognize you?"

"No, I avoided him."

"Anything on Abigail?"

"No. No one I've spoken with has seen or heard anything about her."

You've done well, Jasmine. Let me take over now. Go tell Cobb to meet me here, then head back to the hotel. If you see Wolf, ask him to wait outside the saloon and bring his rifle.

When Cobb arrived, Tasker pointed out the man Jasmine had positively identified. "There are half a dozen jaspers around him. I don't want to cause a fuss in here. I'll move over by the front door. You move to the back, covering the rear. Follow him if he moves. Hopefully, he'll leave alone."

An hour later, Fancy Boots left the saloon, accompanied by five other men who looked more like townies than cowboys. Most of them carried guns, either openly or concealed beneath their clothes. Tasker and Cobb trailed behind them.

As they left the saloon, Wolf caught up with them. Tasker pointed to Fancy Boots. "As soon as they light somewhere, you try to get high and cover us. We don't want to shoot Fancy Boots, but we may have to gun down a few of his friends."

Wolf nodded.

A few buildings down from the Bloody Bucket Saloon was a large horse stable. All six men entered the stalls and began saddling horses as Tasker approached. Fancy Boots was in the stall closest to the door, with an empty stall between him and the others.

Tasker slipped into the stall quietly, one of his guns drawn. He pressed it against Fancy Boots's back and whispered, "Get yer hands up where I can see 'em. Get 'em up about shoulder height. No farther. Good. Now, nice and quiet-like, you're coming with me. If you say anything above a whisper, I'll kill you."

"What's this all about?" Fancy Boots said in a very soft voice. "You got the wrong man, mister."

"I don't think so. Now, let's head out."

"Hell no! I ain't goin' nowhere," he said, almost shouting. Tasker tapped him on the head with the barrel of his revolver hard enough to get his attention. Fancy Boots dropped into a dazed crouch. Tasker holstered his gun, took Fancy Boots under his arm like an old drunk, and began half carrying him out of the stable. Cobb walked backward alongside Tasker, shotgun ready.

"Hold on there!" called a voice from behind. Upon hearing Fancy Boots' shout, his five friends stepped out of their stalls and gathered just outside the stable doors. They lined up in a neat row facing Tasker and Cobb, hands on their guns.

"Where you think yer goin' with Bob?" the tallest one

asked. He was at least a head taller than the other four.

Tasker dropped Bob on the ground, semi-conscious, then faced the five men.

Cobb said, "You'd be smart to stay where you are and take your hands off those hoglegs. We're taking Bob with us." He aimed the shotgun at them and deliberately cocked both hammers, one at a time.

The tallest one looked at Cobb. "There's five of us, says you ain't, and only two of you, lessin' a darky like you can't count so good."

In the brief stillness that followed, an audible click came from above and behind the group. Cobb said, "Count again."

They weren't cowards, but they weren't fools either. One by one, they took their hands off their guns.

Tasker said, "Now get on your horses and ride out of town." The five remained frozen.

"Jefferson, you think they're deciding whether to pull on us? That would be a mistake."

"It would," Cobb said, "but I believe I'd take some pleasure in dismembering this tall loudmouth. What say you?" Cobb brought the shotgun to his shoulder and aimed it directly at the tall one.

There was another split second of silence, then the tall one said, "This ain't over. Get yer horses, boys." The five men retrieved their horses from the stalls and mounted.

Tasker said, "Now, get."

The tall one shouted again, "This ain't over!" as he led the others at a gallop away from the stable, turning a corner about fifty yards down the street.

"That was close," Tasker said, as he picked up Bob, who was still groggy.

"It was," Cobb said.

Wolf, at the doors on the upper level of the stable,

grabbed a rope and slid down to the street. He joined Tasker and Cobb in front of the stable.

"You all right, Snip?" Cobb asked.

"I'm fine," Wolf signed, *"like a summer rain."*

The three detectives began to walk across the street, with Tasker still pulling Bob along. They heard hoofbeats before they saw the riders. The five mounted men, led by the tall one, rounded a corner, charging toward them. Firing pistols from their saddles at fifty yards made them about as effective as throwing rocks.

Tasker dropped Bob and drew his revolver. Cobb put his shotgun in his left hand and drew his Colt with his right. Wolf set his rifle on the ground and drew his own revolver.

The three Pinkertons stood their ground as bullets spattered dirt ineffectively around them. The horsemen were closing in. The three detectives took their time, aimed, and fired almost simultaneously. The tall one and two of his men flew backward off their horses. The other two, seeing their friends fall, abruptly turned their horses and rode off down the street and out of sight.

The shots drew people into the street from various saloons and houses. Before they could gather and ask questions, the trio took Bob into an alley and then to their hotel. As they led Bob past the clerk, Tasker said to him, "Some folks jus' can't hold their whiskey."

The clerk asked, "What was all that shootin' about?"

Tasker said, "Jus' some drunks a hootin' and a hollerin'."

The clerk said, "This town's goin' ta the dogs."

Jasmine was waiting in their room when they burst through the door, Bob in tow. Tasker threw him into a chair. He was starting to recover.

"Now I remember," Jasmine said. "This is Bob Watts. They call him 'Long Hair,' like they used to call Custer. He sold me to Simms, all right. Give me a minute alone with him."

"Not this time," Tasker told her, recalling that she had slit Simms without hesitation. "We need some answers. You go to your room and wait there."

Jasmine stayed still and glared at Tasker. "Now!" Tasker said, angry. Jasmine, clearly upset, left the room.

Watts was slowly regaining his senses. He looked around the room, stopping to stare at Cobb. "Who the hell are you? You the law?"

"No," Cobb said. "Worse."

What Cobb said fit perfectly with the plan Tasker was hatching. He looked menacingly at Watts. "Far worse," he said. "We've been hired to get rid of you."

Tasker's comment caught Wolf off guard, but Cobb picked up on Tasker's game at once. He saw Wolf about to object and immediately silenced him with an open hand and a stern glare.

"Get rid of me? You mean kill me? Who would do that? You're crazy."

"Who do you think?"

"I don't know. You got the wrong guy."

Tasker's tone softened, as if he were reciting lyrical poetry to Watts. "Think about it. Let your mind travel east… all the way east… like New York." Tasker's words and the hypnotic timber of his voice hung in the air.

Watts was thinking, his eyes bulging. "No! That's crazy. I've done everything I've been told to do and more."

"Who have you been talking to, Watts?"

"Nobody! Hell, I don't know enough to tell anyone. I jus' get sent the little whores and sometimes boys, and I place them where they tell me."

"And where's that?" Cobb asked.

"Here, Deming, Silver City, the prettier ones to Las Cruces and El Paso, jus' like I'm told."

"Well, you're sure screwin' it up somewhere, 'cause we don't come cheap." Tasker turned to Cobb. "You want the honors?"

By this time, Wolf had caught on to the scam. Before Cobb could answer, Wolf grabbed him by the arm and signed, *"No. Let me. I'll do it Apache style. Scalp him real good first, then, while he's still alive, cut him twenty or thirty times and watch him slowly bleed to death."* He moved menacingly closer to Watts.

"What the hell's he doin? What was all that hand stuff about?" Watts almost screamed.

"He's talkin' with his hands," Tasker said. "Seems he wants us to do you the Indian way. The Apache way."

Cobb translated Wolf's signing for Watts as Wolf slowly drew his long Arkansas Toothpick and tested the blade for sharpness with his thumb.

Watts shouted, "You can't do that! Wait! No! Can I talk to someone? You gotta let me talk to someone. This is all a mistake!"

"No more talk," Tasker said. "I like the Apache idea. Come on, let's get to it."

Watts's eyes were getting bigger. He was sweating profusely.

Cobb said, "Hold on. You can't do it here." He turned to Watts and pointed at Wolf. "My friend here is half Apache, see, and he gets carried away sometimes. There's too much blood that way. We'd have to take you out, maybe in the Chihuahuan desert somewhere, cut you up, and leave the body for the vultures to feast on. Too much trouble. You ain't worth it."

"That's enough," Tasker said. "I like it. I'd like to see

Wolf-Killer work the Apache way."

Wolf nodded menacingly.

Tasker said, "Let's get him out into the desert before it gets light."

"No, no, no," Watts cried. "Please, I'm beggin' you. I didn't do nothin'. I never said nothin' ta nobody about New York. Hell, I don't know nothin' about 'em… Please."

Cobb said in an even voice, "Ya know… maybe we're bein' too hasty."

"What do ya mean?" Tasker asked, feigning anger toward Cobb.

Cobb turned to Watts. "Look, we know this has something to do with that whore, what was her name?"

"Yeah, I know… Abigail," Tasker said.

"I think the New York bosses liked her. If she vouched he said nothin' ta anybody, maybe…"

"What did ya do with her, Watts?" Tasker asked. "Don't lie to us."

"Abigail? Yeah. We called her Abby. I don't know. Maybe a year ago. Nice lookin' redhead, 'cept somebody messed up her face. She'll tell ya. She'll tell ya I didn't talk ta nobody."

"Where is she now? Maybe she can get you out of this mess," Tasker said.

Watts was trembling. "Yeah, yeah, she's workin' in the Four Aces Saloon in Las Cruces, sure enough. You ask her about me."

"Knock him out," Tasker said.

"Yup," Cobb replied, walking over to where Watts sat. He drew his Colt and struck Watts over the head with the barrel. Watts was knocked out cold.

"Well, that took a while," Tasker said.

"Did," Cobb said. "Now, what are we gonna do with

him? He's not gonna tell us anything else. He's too far down the chain."

Tasker said, "Can't turn him over to the law. They don't have any around here."

In the end, they decided to scare Watts some more and run him out of town. Once he woke up, they told him they would let him go. He was very thankful. However, they warned him to disappear, change his name, and never come back to the Southwest. Watts said he had a cousin in Northern California and promised to go to him and lay low.

Wolf retrieved his horse and saddle from the stable and sent him on his way. Not, however, before he cut a lock of Watts's long hair, telling him it was a trophy to partly make up for his disappointment at not being able to scalp him.

Jasmine forgave Tasker after he explained the game they played with Watts. She seemed disappointed that he was allowed to skedaddle, but she resigned herself to it for the greater good of finding Abigail. She and Tasker spent one last night together under the stars outside Lordsburg before the three detectives headed toward Las Cruces. Before leaving, Tasker gave Jasmine money to take a train back to her home in Kansas City.

"And us," she asked.

"Are you certain there is an 'us'?" Tasker asked.

She kissed him goodbye. "Of course, I am."

"When this assignment is over," he said. "I'll come for you. Then we'll see."

"You'd better, Mister Tasker, or I'll come after you."

Chapter 13

Las Cruces

Las Cruces had grown since the detectives' last visit. Once again, the arrival of the railroad had led to a significant increase in the population, which had reached over 2,000. The buildings were still mostly made of adobe. Since Las Cruces was the county seat of Doña Ana County and there was no town marshal, the Pinkertons pulled up in front of the county sheriff's office.

Tasker and Cobb went inside while Wolf stayed mounted, holding the horses. They found themselves facing an aging lawman, probably over sixty but still fit. The six-pointed star on his chest looked tarnished with age. His hair was long and gray, and he sported a thick, drooping gray mustache that covered his leathery face. On his left hip, rigged for cross draw, sat an old Colt Dragoon revolver.

Tasker and Cobb shared a glance and smiled. Both had the same reaction. The sheriff looked a lot like US Deputy Marshal Waylon Sweet, right down to the old-fashioned pistol he carried. Sweet was a dear friend who had been killed by Indians some time ago.

The sheriff looked up at them from behind his desk. His voice was rough. “I’m Sheriff Roscoe Tidwell. Can I help you?” He didn’t stand, and his voice carried a sharp edge. It appeared that he was not friendly toward strangers.

“We’re with the Pinkerton Agency,” Tasker said. “We’d like your help locating a young lady.”

”We don’t take kindly to Pinks ‘round here,” he said, without explaining the ‘we’ part. “You got badges or somethin’?”

They swung their coats back, revealing their Pinkerton Detective Agency badges.

“What young lady?” he asked.

Tasker described Abigail and then said, “She may be working in a saloon.”

“That whore? Hell, every man in this town knows Abby.”

“Could you point us to her workplace?”

“I could.”

Tasker was getting irritated. *This Jasper might look like Waylon,* he thought*, but I suspect he couldn’t carry Marshal Sweet’s water.*

Tidwell added, “But I think I’ll wait to tell you until after you turn in them guns.”

At that moment, two men wearing Deputy Sheriff’s badges walked into the office. “These here are my deputies, and my kin, Abner and Clem. They’re here in case you decide you don’t want to give over them hog legs.”

Abner and Clem looked like younger versions of the Sheriff, though they seemed a little simple. Clem carried an 8-gauge shotgun slung over his shoulder.

Abner said, “They’s another one outside. Looks like a half-breed ‘pache.”

“Well, bring him on in,” Tidwell said.

Cobb said, “We’re not accustomed to giving up our guns.”

“Well, by damn, ya will today! See, I jus’ don’t like darkies, and I don't like half-breeds, and I especially dislike Pinks." He said the word Pinks like they were something a dog might do on a rug.

Abner entered with Wolf, carrying Wolf's Springfield rifle, Tasker's Winchester, and Cobb's shotgun.

"Now, hand 'em over," Tidwell said. Clem lowered his 8-gauge so it covered the three.

Tasker considered confronting this arrogant lawman and his foolish progeny, but he knew it wouldn't end well either way. It's unwise to fight the law. He unbuckled his gun belt and nodded to Cobb and Wolf, telling them to do the same.

Tidwell said, "You'll find her at the Four Aces Saloon, just a mite farther down the street." He pointed back in the direction they had come from. "Just remember, you Pinks ain't the law here. You got no right to act like it. If ya do, I'm comin' after ya."

They left the Sheriff's Office wishing they hadn't gone there at all.

"I feel undressed," Wolf signed as they walked toward the Four Aces.

"Me too," Tasker said. "So let's get this over with, find Abigail, come back for our guns, and get out of this town. We can't go against the law, even if it's bad."

"Let's," Cobb said.

Wolf nodded.

Tasker entered the saloon first, with Cobb following at a loose distance to cover him. Wolf waited outside. Abigail, or Abby, was there, as Watts and Tidwell said she would be, inside the Four Aces Saloon. The problem was, it was the wrong Abigail—same name, red hair—but instead of a scar, her disfigured face bore a burn that looked like it had been made with a hot flat iron. This slim, nearly naked woman spoke with a strong British accent and clearly enjoyed being a prostitute.

She looked at Tasker hungrily and said, "My name's Abby, love, but I'll be whoever you want me to be."

Tasker thought, *I don't think I'll bother checking for a number twelve carved into this one's ankle.* He said, "Sorry, Abby, maybe next time." She looked disappointed.

As they were leaving the saloon, a voice called out, "That you, Sergeant Major?"

Cobb turned toward a man sitting at a table with his back to the wall near the saloon's door.

"Pat? Is that you?" Cobb asked.

"Sure enough, Sergeant Major, at your service."

"Well, I'll be damned! It is you." He turned to Tasker. "Caleb Tasker, this is Pat Garrett."

"Pleased to meet you," Tasker said, then paused. "The Pat Garrett I've heard so much about? The one who took down the guy they called 'the Kid'?"

"Yeah, that would be me, for my sins."

"Good to see you, Pat," Cobb said. "We've been dealing with this Sheriff Tidwell. You know him?"

"I know him," he said, and it didn't sound friendly toward the Sheriff. He continued, "I'm not a lawman anymore, Sergeant Major, only a rancher. Got a spread over toward Roswell. Came in for supplies. Sit a spell." Tasker and Cobb sat at the table. They moved their chairs to each side of Garrett so their backs were not to the door.

"That sounds tame for you," Cobb said. "As you can see, I'm not a Sergeant Major anymore, either. What's your take on Tidwell?"

"Bad hombre, my friend. You know, back in the day, I might have done some shady things, but Tidwell makes me look like a choirboy. He's the kind who gives lawmen a bad name."

"That's what we figured," Tasker said.

"So, I take it from that badge, you're a Pinkerton now," Garrett said.

Cobb said, "You'd be right...for our sins as well."

"You after somebody hereabouts?"

Cobb told Garrett about their search for Abigail and the human marketers they were trying to find and eliminate.

Garrett was silent for a few moments, then he said, "Sounds like God's work to me. Anything I can do to help? You need a place to stay and work out of?"

"Hell, we've got no leads to follow as it stands," Cobb said. "We don't need a place to stay right now, but we'll take any help we can get. What did you have in mind?"

"I still have plenty of contacts on both sides of the law. Let me spread the word. Can you wait here for maybe a week?"

"You really think you can help?" Tasker asked.

"I do. I have some ideas, and it sounds like these owl hoots need some serious prison time … or maybe a bullet in the back of their heads."

"I think we can tolerate this Tidwell character for a week. What do you say, Caleb?"

"Hell, right now we've got nothing better. Many thanks, Pat," Tasker said as they stood to leave the saloon.

Garrett told Cobb, "I reckon I owe you one, anyway, Sergeant Major. You and your 10th Cav boys pulled my ass out of that Apache ambush a while back."

"Christ, that seems like a lifetime ago. You weren't there that day, Caleb. I recall you had a virus or some such."

"I do remember now," Caleb said. "At least I recall you mentioning it to me. Wasn't it you who told me there were 'hundreds' of Apaches?"

Cobb and Garrett laughed. "Well, maybe it was more like ten or twenty."

"Hell, it seemed like hundreds to this ol' boy," Garrett joked.

Tasker said, "Pleasure meeting you, Mr. Garrett."

"All mine," Garrett said, "and it's Pat." They shook hands.

Garrett added, "Any friend of Sergeant Major Jefferson Cobb is a lifelong friend of mine."

"Pat, it is," Tasker said.

They left the saloon feeling somewhat better but still uneasy without their guns and wondering how long they would have to wait in town with nothing to do. "We'd better get a hotel room if we're gonna be hanging around," Tasker said.

They acquired a room at the Hacienda de Las Cruces Hotel for three people—one large bed for two and a cot, as usual. The hotel was a two-story adobe building with a balcony overlooking the main street. Their room was on the same level as the balcony. When open, their window let in a cool breeze. For more fresh air, they could step onto the balcony, where two reclining chairs were arranged. From there, they could see a good stretch of the main street. The horses were kept at a livery stable around the corner from the hotel.

"At least this is comfortable," Cobb said.

"It is," Tasker said.

Wolf nodded and set his bedroll on the floor next to the empty cot.

Six days after he left, Garrett returned to Las Cruces and met the three detectives again at the small hotel bar.

Cobb made the last introduction. "Pat, this is Sammy Wolf. He's been with us for a few years. The best damn long-range shooter in the territory. I should mention he's also faster and more accurate with a pistol than either Caleb or me."

"My pleasure," Garrett said. "I'm impressed."

"Please tell me you have some news," Tasker said. "If I

stay in this town much longer, I think I'll hang myself."

Pat chuckled. "I don't doubt it. Any more trouble with Tidwell?"

"None," said Cobb. "We've seen him and his two puppies around, but we haven't had any contact. So, what's the news?"

"Well, Sergeant Major, you sure know how to pick your fights. All I could find on this Eastern gang is that they're active across the territory and pretty powerful—thanks to their political connections. Nobody wants to talk about 'em. But the good news is, I think I might have found your Abigail."

Tasker, Cobb, and Wolf—all three—leaned further over the table. Garrett took a sip of the whiskey he had ordered and continued. "You know where Deming is?"

Tasker said, "We rode close by it on the way here from Lordsburg, but avoided going into town."

"Deming has a reputation for being rough, and it's well deserved—no law to speak of. Outlaws run wild in the streets. A good friend of mine was there recently and remembers your Abigail. They called her Abby. Blazing red hair, a faint scar on her right cheek, a real beauty, according to him."

"How recent?" signed Wolf. Cobb translated, adding, "Wolf here doesn't speak much, but he hears exceptionally well."

Garrett looked at Wolf and said, "Hell, speaking's overrated anyway." He smiled at Wolf, who smiled back.

"He says he saw her within the last four weeks. She's working – if that's her – at a saloon. He remembered her because she seemed out of place, too young and too innocent-looking. Especially, the scar seemed odd on such a pretty girl."

"What saloon?" Cobb asked, eager to hear more.

"Guess my friend got really drunk because he couldn't recall the saloon's name. He did say it was near the livery stable in the center of town."

"That sounds promising, really promising," Tasker said. "Well worth following up. Thanks, uh, Pat, thanks."

"My pleasure, gentlemen. Good luck."

After a few drinks, they left Garrett and returned to their room. "We'll light out first thing tomorrow, after we pick up our guns," Tasker said, emphasizing the last part.

Wolf was casually looking out their balcony window. He saw four riders enter town, about to pass right by their hotel. There were three men who looked like *pistoleros*. The fourth rider was a dark-skinned woman, dressed in a town coat and britches, riding her horse like a man. As they drew closer, Wolf's eyes widened. He recognized the woman. *Jasmine should be on a train to her home*, he thought, *not here in Las Cruces*.

"Caleb, Jefferson, you need to see this."

They went to the window.

"That's Jasmine," Tasker almost shouted.

"It is," Cobb echoed. "You think they've got her prisoner?"

"She's not tied up," Wolf said.

"That's odd," Tasker said, dark, unsettling thoughts flickering at the edge of his mind. He said aloud, "If she's with them, why did she slit Simm's throat?" Then he wondered, *Why did she come on to me so strongly? What was all that crap about "us?"*

"Hard to figure," Cobb said. "Maybe her orders and this shooter's came from way above, like from New York or Chicago. Maybe Simms and the other locals were liabilities, and her orders were to kill them all at some point. Maybe when we arrived, it gave her the excuse."

"That's a bunch of maybes, but it doesn't matter," Tasker said. "My money says those *pistoleros* are after us."

"We need to get our guns," Wolf signed in agreement.

"Out the back stairs – move!" Tasker ordered. They left the hotel and hurried through an alley to avoid the shooters, exposed and unarmed.

They burst into the Sheriff's Office and found only Abner, his feet propped on a desk, fast asleep.

Cobb swept Abner's feet off the table. "Our guns!" he said, his tone unmistakable.

"Su...Sure, but Roscoe, I mean the sheriff, says if you pick 'em up, you gotta be out of town by sunset."

"Don't worry. That's our intent. Guns!" Tasker said with equal ferocity.

They left the Sheriff's Office, strapping on their sidearms and loading cartridges from their belts. They stopped by the stable to saddle the horses, just in case. Cobb tucked his shotgun into its scabbard. Tasker and Wolf also left their rifles behind.

Tasker said, "Let's head to the hotel. We'll check out, then go after those shooters and Jasmine."

They hurried toward the hotel. Wolf saw them first. Jasmine and two gunmen were on the balcony outside their hotel room window. "Up there!" he yelled. Tasker and Cobb saw them.

Jasmine shouted, "There they are!" as she pointed at the three Pinkertons. The two shooters immediately opened fire from the balcony, and the third fired from the open window. Jasmine stood with them, her gun blazing. Tasker and Cobb saw Jasmine firing. Tasker was now certain he knew the terrible truth.

She's one of them. His thoughts were swirling. *It all makes sense now. She was tied up when they found the wag-*

on, probably because Simms didn't know she worked for the Eastern bosses. She cut Simms' throat because that was her orders. She came on to me to find out how close we were to her bosses. How could I have been such a fool?

As these thoughts raced through his mind, Tasker took cover behind a barrel and opened fire on the group on the balcony. Cobb and Wolf ducked behind a water trough and returned fire. A bullet passed through Tasker's left side, lightly wounding him. A bullet grazed Wolf's right ear. The gunman firing from inside the hotel room was hit and vanished. Jasmine was wounded and fell hard, clutching her stomach. The other two *pistoleros* on the balcony retreated back into the room where they had been standing.

Tasker was running toward the hotel but stumbled, clutching his side. Cobb and Wolf caught up to him and burst through the hotel doors into the lobby. It looked empty. All patrons and staff had taken cover after hearing the gunfire.

The two remaining gunmen yelled as they hurried down the wide stairs from the second floor to the lobby. Wolf shot one in the head, and he fell dead halfway down. Cobb shot the other gunman, who dropped his pistol and tumbled down the stairs. Both of his hands were over his groin, and he was moaning.

Tasker, ignoring the pain in his side and the bloodstain slowly spreading across his shirt, cut between Cobb and Wolf. He ran up the stairs past the dead gunman. On the balcony, he cradled Jasmine in his arms. She was alive, barely.

Tasker said her name, "Jasmine."

Her eyes fluttered open. She smiled and said, "Caleb, I am sorry. Be careful. This is bigger than you can imagine." Her mouth went slack, and with glazed, open eyes, she died in Caleb's arms. He stayed with her for a few minutes, his mind frozen and empty, unable to grasp her betrayal or her death. Then he gently carried her through the hotel room and down the stairs to the lobby.

Sheriff Tidwell and his deputies, having heard the gunfire, were already in the lobby, waiting with Cobb, Wolf, and the wounded gunmen. The local doctor, carrying his medical bag and accompanied by a woman, ran forward to meet Tasker. They took Jasmine's body from Tasker's arms.

For the first time, Tasker noticed that Cobb and Wolf were in handcuffs. Still shaken by Jasmine's death, he said nothing and stared at them.

The wounded gunman shouted, "That's him, Sheriff. Look what he done to me. My pards and I, and my woman, were on the balcony, tending our business. These bastards started shootin' for no reason. Two of my pards are dead, and that beautiful lady. They gotta pay." By now, the doctor was working on the bullet wound in the crotch of the gunman who screamed in agony.

"Well, well. Looks like you boys don't listen to good advice," Tidwell rasped.

Cobb said, "This is ridiculous. There were four of them against three of us. They were in our room and on the balcony. It was an ambush. They opened fire as soon as they saw us."

Tasker was silent.

"So you say," Tidwell looked pleased with himself as he snapped the cuffs on Tasker.

"Lock 'em up, Abner, and be careful. I hear them Pinks are tough hombres." His laughter filled the lobby.

Later that night, the doctor arrived at the Sheriff's Office, which also served as the jail. He cleaned Tasker's wound and Wolf's ear. Tasker sat on his cot in the small cell, gazing at the walls, the floor, or the bars. Except for brief responses when Cobb or Wolf tried to start a conversation, he remained silent.

Tidwell was resolute. He told his deputies, "You don't let nobody talk to these three. Nobody, till the Judge comes. It should be about two weeks he's due. Enjoy your stay, *pendejos*." As an afterthought, he added, "And no telegrams either. No sending or receiving."

"We need to get out of here, Caleb. This sheriff will have us hanged," Cobb said that night.

Tasker, still despondent, replied, "Yeah, we have to."

The next day, they discovered the full extent of Sheriff Tidwell's cruelty. It revealed itself through six massive Mexicans who appeared out of nowhere, though it was obvious Tidwell had summoned them. Abner and Clem took the three Pinkertons, shackled at wrists and ankles, behind the sheriff's office into a yard enclosed by a tall, sturdy wooden fence, hidden from curious passersby. This area was typically used to give prisoners some open space once a day. There was also a solid, locked door leading out of the yard. The six Mexicans waited with clubs. The three Pinkertons couldn't defend themselves and were severely beaten, though the Mexicans made sure not to hit their faces. They mainly targeted Tasker, since Tidwell particularly disliked him.

Back in their cell, Tasker was groggy and silent. Cobb asked, "You hurt bad?"

"No more than you," he replied. "What about Wolf?"

"I'm fine," Wolf said through clenched teeth, pressing his side. Because he was more frail than Tasker or Cobb, the beating had taken a heavier toll on his body.

"They haven't done any real damage yet," Cobb said, "but we can't take much more of this."

Three days later, Tidwell ordered the second round, but this time the Pinkertons were prepared. Even Tasker snapped out of his doldrums when he realized these Mexicans could kill one or more of them without anyone finding out. He was especially worried about Wolf, whose ribs were clearly broken.

When Abner and Clem arrived with the shackles, Cobb said, "Not today, assholes." He hit Abner once, knocking him to the ground. Then, in one swift move, he grabbed Clem's shotgun and trained it on both deputies. Tidwell, in the outer office, heard the commotion. He came through the door, running into Cobb and the shotgun. He stopped abruptly.

"On your knees," Tasker said, now holding Abner's revolver. He cocked the gun and pressed the barrel against Tidwell's chest. Tidwell obeyed, fear clear on his face.

Cobb stepped out behind the sheriff's office and came right back. "Our Mexican friends have taken off, gone in all directions. Guess you're on your own, Sheriff."

"Please don't kill me," he croaked, trembling.

"To think we thought this piece of dung was like Waylon Sweet," Cobb said, leaning down to come face-to-face with Tidwell. "Why, you're not worth the sweat on his balls. Caleb, how 'bout you go wire our headquarters while I decide whether I'm gonna kill this poor excuse for a human?"

Cobb's shotgun replaced Tasker's revolver, pressing against Tidwell's forehead. Tasker nodded and left the office without a word. He hurried to the railroad station, where he wired Pinkerton Headquarters, explaining their situation as best he could. The reply simply said, '*Stand by.' Don't do anything reckless. Sending a lawyer now. I'll be there as soon as I can – Buford.*

Tasker returned to the sheriff's office and told Cobb and Wolf the results. "I think that means we shouldn't try to break out of jail," he said.

"Yep. Damn shame," Cobb replied, "but we don't have a choice unless we want to become fugitives."

Wolf nodded in agreement.

Cobb looked at Tidwell. "Get up! We're gonna make a

deal. See, our bosses know what's happened here. We're gonna give you back your weapons and return to our cell until the judge gets here. You're gonna treat us with respect until that judge arrives, or we'll see to it that everybody from here to the big ocean knows how you were made to grovel before the Pinkerton Agency in your own jail. Our Agency will ensure the story reaches the world. You'll have to go to China to get peace. Understood? If you agree, the story will go no further. Nod your heads if you understand."

Tidwell and both his deputies nodded. Cobb, Wolf, and Tasker removed the bullets from their guns, then walked them back into their cell.

"You think he'll live up to it?" Tasker asked. His voice was flat, giving Cobb the impression he didn't care either way.

"Humf ..." Cobb said. "I think he might for the next few days, when hopefully the lawyer or Buford will be here, and, with luck, the judge."

"Thanks, Jefferson. I was pretty worthless."

"You were," Cobb answered.

CHAPTER 14

THE TRIAL

Two days later, unbeknownst to the detectives still locked in their cell, a small man named Frank Cage arrived in town and registered at the Hacienda de Las Cruces Hotel. He told the clerk he was in town to defend the three men in jail for murder. The clerk felt it his duty to immediately inform Sheriff Tidwell, who then sent Abner and Clem to speak with Mr. Cage. They found him in his hotel room. An hour later, Cage checked out of the hotel with all his belongings. He walked out with Abner and Clem, each holding one of his arms. He was never seen again.

Judge Hiram Baker arrived in Las Cruces a few days later during his circuit of the territory. There was still no sign of Buford Cartwright.

Tidwell had regained some of his bravado. He believed he still had a chance to put these Pinkertons in their place. He explained to Judge Baker with firm conviction.

"These three murdered two men and a girl and badly wounded another, Judge," Tidwell pronounced. "I got me an eyewitness, my two deputies as witnesses, the bodies, the guns that did it, the works. Real short trial, I'm guessin', then we hang 'em."

"You sound very convinced," Judge Baker said. The Judge was a large, barrel-chested man, dressed in black and wearing a top hat.

"You want I should start buildin' the scaffold?"

"These are Pinkerton men, is that right, Tidwell?" He did not call him "sheriff."

"Yeah, that's right."

"I find it hard to believe, Tidwell. I've heard about these men. I'm told they have excellent reputations. Why, Tasker is a West Point graduate, a Captain in the 10th Cavalry, and Cobb is a retired Sergeant Major in the 10th."

"That's as it may be, but they're still murderin' scum. I got 'em, cold as a Wyoming winter."

This happened during the day at the same hotel where I am staying, right?

"Yup."

"Then there should be plenty more eyewitnesses than one, especially if he's one of the participants in the fracas, and your deputies, according to the statements I read, arrived on the scene after it was over."

"Maybe, Judge. But, trust me, you don't need ta go no further. This is a sure thing."

"Yes. Well, I think I'll do some checking anyway."

Tidwell muttered to himself as he walked off.

Judge Baker sensed that something was wrong. He spoke with many hotel staff and townspeople present that day. He learned from the hotel clerk that the last people to see Frank Cage were Abner and Clem Tidwell. The clerk also signed a sworn statement stating that when Cage left the hotel with the two deputies, he had a black eye and his clothes were disheveled.

Baker spoke with Sheriff Tidwell and his deputies. The

sheriff said he had only welcomed Cage to Las Cruces. Abner and Clem Tidwell said they thought Cage had rented a horse somewhere because the last time they saw him, he was riding out of town with his valise tied to the saddle.

Baker sent a telegram to the Pinkerton Agency, and two days later, a man named Buford Cartwright telegraphed him to say that a Pinkerton lawyer named Cage had been sent to Las Cruces and should already be there. Buford also vouched for the detectives and mentioned that personal problems were delaying him, but he would soon be on his way.

The following day, he received a telegram directly from William Pinkerton indicating his high regard for the three detectives.

The trial began as soon as the wounded gunman, Jack Collier, the supposed eyewitness, was able to testify. The town had converted the Hacienda de Las Cruces Hotel lobby into a courtroom, complete with a judge's bench, spectator seats, a jury box, and a witness stand. By the time the court opened, the seats were filled to capacity with early arrivals, and the entire lobby was thick with cigar and pipe smoke. Tidwell's deputies stood guard at the door, and Jack Collier, in a wheelchair with bandages covering his crotch, sat among the spectators.

Buford Cartwright was present, along with Pat Garrett and several of his hired hands. Tidwell had not allowed either Cartwright or Garrett to consult with the 'prisoners' before the trial. The attorney appointed by Tidwell for the defendants was ineffective; therefore, Judge Baker began by telling him to sit down and stay quiet. The man was confused but obeyed.

Tasker, Cobb, and Wolf were led in wearing handcuffs. The crowd's muttering grew louder as they arrived, creating a constant background noise. As they passed Cartwright and

Garrett, Cobb shouted, "I am happy to see you both. Thanks for coming. Your lawyer never showed."

"I know," Cartwright shouted back. "He apparently came to the hotel here in town but has since gone missing."

"Tidwell?" Cobb asked, but was forced to keep walking.

"We'll talk later." Buford was still yelling over the chaos of everyone in the lobby talking at once.

Tasker nodded to them and smiled as he passed, but said nothing. As the senior detective in the trio, he surprised both Cartwright and Garrett with his apparent detachment.

Judge Baker hammered his gavel three times on the makeshift bench and said loudly and clearly, "This will not be a jury trial. Any rulings made today will be mine alone."

Tidwell was surprised by the judge's words. *I'm the prosecutor*, he thought. He was, in fact, acting as the prosecutor because no qualified lawyer was available. He figured he'd better move this along, so he stood up to call his first witness, Collier, to the stand.

"I'd like to call Jack Coll – "

Judge Baker cut him off, slamming his gavel on the desk. "Tidwell, sit yourself down."

"But yer Honor."

"Sit! Now!" Tidwell grumbled as he sat.

Judge Baker began. "I have a few things to say. First, Sheriff Tidwell, I'm officially informing you that I've been in touch with the Territorial Governor, the Honorable Edmund G. Ross, who is my cousin, by the way. He has assured me he will be looking closely at your competence to continue as Sheriff of Doña Ana County."

"What? Why?" Tidwell shouted, standing up again.

"Shut up! Sit!" Judge Baker barked. "I'm talking. Do not interrupt me again, or I'll throw you in your own jail."

Tidwell sat back down, eyes wide, mouth closed.

The Judge continued, "I've spent the past few days investigating this incident myself. I've interviewed most of the staff at this hotel, especially those who were actually there on the day of the incident. I've also talked to half a dozen townsfolk who saw firsthand what happened that day. All of them tell the same story."

He looked directly at Tidwell. "I conclude that the defendants here today were fired upon first from the balcony, and responded only after bullets were flying toward them and kicking up dust around their feet. I have sworn statements to back my conclusion."

Tidwell was now squirming in his chair, looking pale.

"Furthermore, I've interviewed Mr. Jack Collier, the Sheriff's eyewitness, and I find his story highly unlikely. More accurately, it's a pack of damn lies. Additionally, for your information, Sheriff, I have discovered, quite easily, I might add, that this man Collier is wanted for robbery and the murder of a seventy-year-old widow in Abilene, Texas. He will be held for the Texas Rangers, who are en route."

Collier began edging his wheelchair toward the back of the lobby.

"I also have strong evidence," Baker continued, "that your two deputies kidnapped and possibly murdered a Pinkerton Agency attorney named Frank Cage. No doubt under your orders. I'll allow the Rangers to take you, Tidwell, but I've called in a Deputy U.S. Marshal to investigate your deputies. They will be held with you, in your jail, pending his arrival."

Sheriff Tidwell stood shocked and frozen. His two deputies sat wide-eyed in their seats.

"Will the defendants please stand?" Judge Baker said.

Tasker, Cobb, and Wolf stood up. They were no longer sullen, but stunned and hopeful. Even Tasker began to smile.

Judge Baker looked at each of them individually. "The case is dismissed! You gentlemen are free to go, and the court apologizes for the sheriff's detention of you in the first place."

Cartwright approached the trio with a key given to him by Judge Baker and unlocked the detectives' handcuffs. Pat Garrett and half a dozen of his ranch hands had moved to the hotel doors behind Abner and Clem. Two stood behind Tidwell, and two more stood behind Collier, whose wheelchair was almost at the lobby entrance.

Judge Baker said, "Mr. Garrett, I hereby temporarily swear you and your hands in as Deputy City Marshals of Las Cruces. You are authorized to apprehend and incarcerate Tidwell, Collier, and the two deputies in the back for making false statements, interfering with the course of justice in my damned court, murder, conspiracy to murder, and any other damned thing I can think of."

"Our pleasure, Your Honor," Garrett said. He nodded, and his ranch hands took custody of the culprits.

That night, Pat Garrett, his hands, Cobb, Wolf, Cartwright, and Judge Baker celebrated in the hotel bar. Tasker was not with them and could not be found. He rode off on Blaze immediately after the court adjourned.

The next morning, Judge Baker, Cartwright, and Garrett left Las Cruces. Garrett and his men rode on horseback, while the Judge and Cartwright traveled by train. Tasker hadn't returned yet.

"What do you think?" signed Wolf.

"You mean about Caleb?" Cobb asked, already knowing the answer.

"Of course."

"He needs some time, is all. There are things you don't know, Sammy."

"What things?"

"Maybe it's time you knew the rest anyway. Caleb's had some pretty bad luck with women."

"I know about Sarah, and now Jasmine. What else?"

"The first woman Caleb truly loved. Back East, where he's from, and during the war. The woman he was supposed to marry stole all his savings and ran off with some sportin' man."

"What happened?"

"You know Caleb. He tracked 'em down in some hotel room, damn near killed both of 'em, and got his money back. It hit him hard as nails, though. He really loved that woman. He couldn't shake it for a long time. Even when I first met him in the cavalry, he was moody, sullen, and distant. He always kept close counsel. I understood it and knew I had to leave him alone sometimes. Well, in Serpent's Creek, Sarah brought him out of it. I think he fell deeply in love again. Then he thought she'd betrayed him like his fiancée did – you remember on the trail in Texas?"

"Yeah, she was a prisoner for a while, but it turned out she didn't betray him, didn't it?"

"It did, but about the time he figured that out, she was brutally killed right in front of him. He never got to tell her. Blames himself. He thinks he should have trusted her more and figured it out sooner. After that, when he finally came back to the living, he was plainly off women. Polite, always polite, but kept his distance. Stuck to being with the odd whore with no attachments. Then he comes across Jasmine, and she plum seduces him, and it begins all over again. I think Jasmine was the worst. Pure evil, you ask me."

"What does that mean, the worst?"

"He loved her more deeply than the others. Her betrayal has really gotten to him, bad. We need to give him time to work it out."

"I can do that," Wolf signed. *"He's the closest thing to a father I've ever had."*

"I know, Snip."

It wasn't easy. Tasker returned in a day or two, clothes filthy, hair unkempt, and a scruffy beard beginning to grow. He stayed in his room for days and spent his nights in saloons, drinking until he was too drunk to walk. Cobb or Wolf usually carried him back to his hotel bed late at night. His beard grew longer, and he became more irritable around others, even Cobb and Wolf. They stayed loyal, giving him space, hoping he'd find his way again. He still replied to them with short, abrupt sentences, often tinged with indifference.

Their ongoing search for Lawyer Cage's body proved fruitless. Tidwell and his deputies maintained their story that he had simply vanished. Tasker appeared indifferent. During such moments, Cobb would ask, "You with us?"

Tasker's answer was usually short and to the point. "I'm fine, God Damn it! Leave me the hell alone."

Tasker started fights in the saloons around Las Cruces. There still wasn't a lawman to replace Tidwell, so Cobb mostly took on that role, with Wolf as his deputy. The townsfolk seemed to accept this setup, as the town remained peaceful under Cobb and Wolf's leadership. However, that meant Cobb had to handle the troubles and misunderstandings Tasker caused, as the increasingly drunken fool.

This continued for several weeks. One night, for no clear reason, Tasker started a fight in a saloon and nearly killed a man. The brawl spilled into the street. Amid the chaos, Tasker's Colt slipped from its holster into the dirt. A ten-year-old Mexican boy, who had been watching the fight, picked it up. The boy ran into an alley and began playing with the gun while Tasker was still struggling with the man outside the alley.

A loud gunshot from the alley froze everything in place. This happened as Cobb arrived at the scene of the fight. Cobb ran into the alley, followed by Tasker, who was partly sobered by the chaos and the gunshot. The stunned boy sat with his back against a wall in the alley, holding the smoking gun with both hands between his splayed legs. On the opposite wall of the alley was a .45 bullet hole in a bakery, which was luckily closed.

"My God," said Tasker. "That's my gun. What the hell have I done?"

Cobb carefully took the Colt from the shocked boy and handed it to Tasker. "You could have killed this boy, Caleb. You think you can keep this in its holster?"

Tasker stared at Cobb. What he saw in his best friend's eyes, the eyes of the man he'd been in so many tight places with, was disgust. Tasker holstered his revolver, slid the leather retention tab over the Colt's hammer, turned, and walked away.

He returned to the hotel room they shared. No one was there. He shaved, combed his hair, brushed off his clothes, cleaned his boots, threw his whiskey flask in the trash, and waited.

Cobb and Wolf entered together, surprised to see Tasker dressed and waiting. The three of them looked at each other for nearly a full minute, with no words exchanged.

Then Tasker said, "Let's resupply, then let's go find Abigail; she's been out there for too long."

Chapter 15

Abigail

The three Pinkerton detectives had passed near the town of Deming, Grant County, New Mexico Territory, weeks earlier on their journey from Lordsburg to Las Cruces. They did not enter Deming for very good reasons. Instead, they had camped only one night, far enough away to avoid the town.

Deming was nestled not so quietly about halfway between Lordsburg and Las Cruces. It was expected to become a thriving railroad town where the Atchison, Topeka & Santa Fe Railroad intersected with the Southern Pacific Railroad. It was supposed to be a hub for supply and support for the many silver, gold, copper, and zinc mining operations around Silver City in the north and Lordsburg farther west. However, it did not meet those expectations.

The railroad was built by 1881, when Deming was founded; however, the town was considered wild and lawless, populated by outlaws, troublemakers, rowdy saloons, and gambling joints. There was no Grant County Sheriff or Deming Town Marshal. Those who took either job did not last long. The last lawman was a Deputy U.S. Marshal sent by the Territorial Governor to restore peace to the town. He lasted only two days. An unknown scoundrel ambushed him with an 8-gauge shotgun, nearly blowing him in half.

The three Pinkertons resupplied in Las Cruces, then retraced their route back to Deming. Tasker, though still not very talkative, was mostly his usual self. They learned about Deming's reputation as they rode into the busy town a few days later.

If they hadn't known the town's character, it was instantly apparent once they entered. The streets were crowded with people jostling one another. Two drunks staggered out of a saloon, fighting in the street until one drew a revolver and shot the other in the chest.

"You see that?" Cobb asked as they rode three abreast down the main street.

"No one hardly reacts. No law. Bad news," Tasker almost shouted above the din. "You smell that?"

"What did you say? Can't hear myself think."

"What's that smell?"

"Yeah, the whole town smells like one big garbage dump." Cobb wrinkled his nose. Wolf pinched his nose and blinked.

"Lovely," Tasker replied. "There's a stable yonder. Let's put the horses up and get started. This is gonna be a bit dicey."

They instructed the stableman to leave their horses saddled.

"Loosen the cinch and feed them," Wolf signed. Tasker translated the sign.

The Pinkertons moved onto the main street, ready for trouble and a quick escape if needed. Cobb brought his shotgun, but Wolf left his rifle with the stable attendant for safekeeping. He was as skilled with his Colt revolver at close range as with his rifle at a thousand yards, and he was quick. This time, their badges were clearly visible, peeking out from their coats.

Trouble broke out immediately. Forcing their way into the Ambrosia Saloon, the one closest to the stable in the middle of town, they were confronted by half a dozen miners. The miners rose from their tables around the room and formed a cluster, blocking the lawmen's path.

They stood there, glaring at the detectives. No words were exchanged.

"Excuse me, gentlemen," Tasker said.

One of the miners wearing a soft cap with an oil-wick lamp on the front said, "You ain't welcome here."

"Why not?" Tasker asked.

"Three reasons. We don't like darkies, we don't like half-breeds, and we particularly don't like Pinkertons."

Tasker sighed, thinking of Sheriff Tidwell and others. "We're hearing a lot of that lately. So, you want to do this with guns or fists?"

"You gonna take on the whole room?" the miner laughed.

"No, just you," Cobb said, moving around Tasker and raising his shotgun. "You won't live through it either way." He cocked the shotgun.

The miner blinked, surprised by the reaction. Cobb's shotgun indicated that more than one miner would be hit by the first two barrels. Some of the other miners began calmly returning to their seats.

The talkative miner lowered his head, stepped back, and signaled the Pinkertons into the saloon. His fellow miners moved aside, giving the detectives room. The three lawmen headed to the bar. Tasker and Wolf faced the bartender, while Cobb stood behind them, casually holding a cocked shotgun across his chest.

The bartender, a weathered-looking character, had seen

better days. He looked old and sluggish, yet he knew his craft. "What'll it be, gents?"

"Some information," Tasker said. He described Abigail.

The bartender knew immediately. "That's Abby. Pretty little thing. She's no longer in town. She did really well around here, but I think she got into trouble with her boss. She was here one day, gone the next. Rumor has it that a mining company up north bought her from the Silver Dollar Saloon, where she worked. She was a real find out here. Beautiful red hair and a body that'd make a padre forget his prayers."

"You talk too much," Tasker said, grabbing the now-frightened barman by his shirt. "Where is she?"

"Hey, I'm tryin' ta help you. Truth is, she got herself beat up real bad by a customer, so they sold her to the mining camp fellas. Word is she's working the mining camps around Silver City. They're bad places, mister. I wouldn't go there if I were you."

"Who are the 'they' you're talking about, the ones who sold her?"

"The saloon owner where she worked… the Silver Dollar."

Their presence and purpose had apparently spread, and they had no similar trouble with miners at the Silver Dollar. They asked for the owner, and a small, bald man in a wrinkled pinstriped town coat cautiously approached them.

"I suspect you know why we're here," Tasker said.

"Yer lookin' fer Abby, right?" He sounded Irish.

"That's right, but first, who did you buy her from?"

"I can't tell ya that. They'd have my guts fer garters."

Cobb stepped in, shoved the little man into the bar, and forced his teeth open with his shotgun barrels, pushing them into the man's mouth. "I won't care about your guts if you don't stop jerkin' us around. I'll blow yer damned head off."

"Ork … arg …" the man mumbled. Cobb took the barrels out. The man blurted, "I'll tell ya, Jesus wept, ya don't need ta be doin' that. I'll tell ya."

"Talk to us," Tasker said.

"She's at the big mining camp at Chloride Flat, jus' west of Silver City, in a saloon. It ain't got no name, says 'Saloon' above the door. Them miners love Abby. Yer not about ta take her easy, no sir."

"That's our problem," Cobb said, smashing his shotgun butt into the man's face, breaking most of his front teeth. "And her name's Abigail." They left the saloon owner bleeding all over his bar.

They retrieved their horses from the stable and rode off quickly from Deming. "I'm mighty glad we're on horseback," Tasker said as they headed north.

"Yup," replied Cobb.

Wolf nodded, leaning forward, patting Wind's neck as they trotted along the trail.

Chloride Flat Camp wasn't much of a camp; there was an adobe shack marked 'Saloon,' a mercantile store, and a vast scattering of tents in every direction. They decided to place Wolf on a rise overlooking the saloon entrance and within easy rifle range.

They entered the saloon together and stopped inside, one to the left and one to the right of the doors. This time, their badges were not visible. The room was dimly lit, but they spotted Abigail immediately. She was standing in front of what seemed to be a small, curtained-off area at the back of the room. Abigail, frail and undernourished, wore only a dirty white cotton chemise, soiled linen pantalets, and black stockings, with no shoes. Her long red hair hung in messy, wild curls. Despite all that, her beauty still shone through.

The place was larger inside than it appeared from the outside, and it was packed with miners—all drunk or well on their way. Most wore soft hats with oil-wick lamps attached to the front. In the saloon, at least two men dressed like cowhands looked out of place among the grimy miners. They seemed to be bouncers. Each wore a brimmed hat, a vest, and trousers tucked into knee-high boots. Each carried a low-hung revolver at the right hip.

Like a picturesque potentate, a very small man sat in an ornate chair atop a table just a few yards from the makeshift room where Abigail stood. He wore a fancy frock coat and a bowler hat. No more than five feet tall, he had what appeared to be proportionately stubby arms and legs. He waved both hands around, praising the virtues of 'Miss Abby.' Tasker and Cobb immediately identified him as the 'boss.' His attire and demeanor were too unusual not to be.

"I make that little person over there, Abigail's procurer and the owner of this operation, wouldn't you say, Jefferson?"

"I would," Cobb replied as they both headed straight for the seated fancy-man. Even while seated on a chair atop a table, Cobb could almost look the man in the eye.

Cobb arrived first. The short man waved his right hand in an exaggerated circular motion and said in a somewhat high-pitched voice, "Ah, my tall, dark Prince, what pleasures can I find for you this magical night? Oh, and for your less-tall friend as well?"

"Can I assume you are the owner of this fine establishment?" Cobb asked, with feigned formality.

"That would be accurate. I am, indeed, Alonso Smith, the proprietor, *à votre service*."

"And do you possess this fair maiden I behold?" Cobb asked, pointing at Abigail.

"Indeed, I do," said Alonso Smith. "Would you like to partake of her enormous pleasures?"

"Not really," Tasker interrupted. "We actually want to buy her from you."

Alonzo laughed. "I'm afraid she's not for sale, not at any price."

"I think you'll find that is not so," Tasker said quietly, placing a one-dollar silver coin on the tiny man's knee.

Alonzo laughed again. "This is a joke, yes?"

"This is a joke, no!" Cobb said as he subtly drew his shotgun from beneath his coat and aimed both barrels at the edge of the coin, pointing at Alonzo's privates.

Amid the noise and chaos in the saloon, no one saw or heard what was happening between Cobb, Tasker, and Mr. Smith. Only Abigail noticed. She began to panic when she saw the shotgun.

The now terrified Alonzo Smith cried, "Take her. Take her. No whore is worth this."

"Keep your voice down, little man," Cobb said. "My finger aches to be pulled, and it kinda has a mind of its own."

Tasker motioned to Abigail with a hand gesture. She moved hesitantly, her eyes wide and her mouth trembling. Tasker whispered, "Relax, Abigail. Everything's going to be all right. We've come from your brother Micky to take you out of this place. You must do exactly what I say, exactly."

"Micky? I don't understand. How could you… ?"

"No time for talk. We call him Micky, but he said to say we know you call him Michael. We need to move. If you resist, I'll knock you out and carry you. Now, will you come along?"

"Yes," she said simply, regaining her composure.

Cobb warned Alonzo, "You're coming too. My shotgun's right under my coat. One wrong word or signal to your henchmen, and I'll blow your cock off...first...then your head if there's time. Understand?"

"I do."

Alonzo carefully climbed down from his perch, and the group moved toward the saloon's only exit, through the chaotic crowd. Tasker was first, gripping Abigail's arm. Alonzo was second, with Cobb close behind, the double-barreled shotgun pressed against Alonzo's lower back.

They were nearly at the saloon door when one of the henchmen shouted, "Hey, boss, where are you going?"

Cobb jabbed the shotgun deeper into Alonzo's back. Alonzo said, "Going for a breath of air, Simon, not to worry." Simon did not answer, but Tasker swung the saloon door open, and they left the saloon behind.

It was nearly dark. Blaze and Two-Socks were tied nearby, and the others hurried toward them. Before they could reach their mounts, a voice behind them shouted, "Stop right there, you bastards." It was Simon, the henchman, and his partner outside the saloon, guns drawn. Tasker, Abigail, and Cobb froze, then turned to face the danger. Alonzo Smith jerked away from Cobb's shotgun and ran behind the two gunmen. Angry saloon patrons began gathering behind them, grumbling about being disturbed while they were drinking.

"You are both fools," Alonzo shrieked. "The name 'Simon' is, of course, not his real name. It's a code that means I'm in trouble. Now you're going to die, except for the girl. None of these fine gentlemen behind me would ever let Abby go."

He yelled to the growing crowd, "They're trying to kidnap Abby, boys! Are we gonna let that happen?" The crowd grumbled louder, some drawing pistols.

Tasker whispered to Abigail, "When I say the word, I'll get on my horse and pull you up behind me."

Abigail nodded.

"Wait for it," Tasker said with confidence.

Alonzo was still ranting, "We should hang 'em! Are you with me?" The crowd was starting to shout their approval when a single loud crack split the air. The man called Simon's head exploded. Pieces of skin, bone, and hair covered many of the crowd. They were frozen in place.

Tasker said, "Now!"

He and Cobb mounted. Tasker pulled Abigail up behind him. A second shot rang out, and this time, the other henchman was knocked off his feet, dead where he lay. The crowd was now running for their lives, except for Alonzo, who was chasing after their fleeing horses. He screamed gibberish as he stumbled after them. When Cobb looked back, he saw the small man falter, out of breath, with one arm raised, aiming a revolver. A third shot rang out, and Alonzo Smith crumpled to the ground.

They rode well out of gunshot range and were soon joined by Wolf, who was smiling.

"Nice work, Snip," Cobb said.

"What's that you're dragging behind you?" Tasker asked.

Wolf beamed, then signed, *"Why, it's a horse, of course, saddled and ready for Miss Abigail. It was lying around unattended while I was getting into position, so I borrowed it."*

"Very thoughtful, Sammy." He turned to Abigail. "This is our Abigail. Abigail, this is Sammy Wolf, the best damn shot in the West."

"Howdy, Miss Abigail," Wolf signed. Tasker translated it.

Abigail smiled at Wolf but said nothing. She nimbly dismounted Blaze and mounted Wolf's borrowed horse. It was a plain gray saddle horse that looked sturdy. It was obvious that Abigail could ride by the way she grabbed the reins and took charge of the animal.

They rode across country, more or less toward Serpent's

Creek, at a slow trot. Tasker asked, "Why did you come along so willingly, Abigail? At first, you seemed mighty scared."

Abigail explained, "No one else could have known my brother's nickname, Micky, and that I always called him Michael. Besides," she blushed, "I liked your face."

It was Tasker's turn to blush. "Uh...uh...We're taking you to meet your brother and the family he lives with. They're the Pembrooks, lovely folks, and they'll be happy to meet you and look after you. Michael treats them like parents. I'll send a telegram to have them meet us in Albuquerque or Santa Fe."

"Oh god, I can't meet them like this. I'm filthy and practically naked." That wasn't entirely true, though, because Wolf gave her his town coat to make her look more presentable and keep her warm at night.

Tasker said, "You can get fully cleaned up and have fresh clothes from friends of ours in Serpent's Creek. We'll spend the night there, then catch a train the next day."

The Abbotts, especially Savannah, warmly welcomed them. Mrs. Rebeccah Abbott immediately took charge of Abigail, bathing her, fixing her hair, and selecting a suitable dress from Savannah's closet. Abigail looked and felt like a new person.

Tasker sent a telegram to the Pinkerton Agency in Albuquerque to report Abigail's discovery. He also sent a telegram to Clarence Pembrook, requesting that they meet in Albuquerque or Santa Fe to reunite Abigail with her brother, Micky.

The Agency's reply was, "Good work. Carry on."

Clarence Pembrook's reply was detailed and full of praise. Mr. and Mrs. Pembrook and Micky would meet them in five days in Albuquerque. It continued: *Hello and best wishes to our Abigail. We look forward to meeting soon—love from Clarence, Mavis, and Michael.*

The telegram brought Abigail to tears. Savannah's mother, Rebeccah, however, was skilled at comforting her.

It took almost a week, but Abigail gradually emerged from the protective shell she had built around herself to survive. Savannah helped by letting Abigail try on dresses from her closet. They fit perfectly with a few minor alterations by Mrs. Abbott.

Savannah gladly gave her a few of them and provided a chest to pack them in. Savannah and her mother also styled Abigail's hair in a manner she truly loved. Before long, the two young ladies were acting as if they had been friends for years, and Abigail was calling Mrs. Abbott 'Auntie Becca'.

By the time they were ready to leave for Albuquerque, Abigail and Savannah were like sisters. They promised to meet again very soon. At the train station, they hugged and cried.

It was a one-day train ride to Albuquerque for Tasker, Cobb, and Abigail. Wolf stayed in Serpent's Creek, in the caring and protective arms of Savannah. Blaze and Two-Socks rode in a livestock car, while Tasker, Cobb, and Abigail traveled in a passenger car attached to it.

Chapter 16

The Reunion

Abigail sat beside Tasker. The train heading north to Albuquerque rattled over a rough patch. The jarring motion of the passenger car was almost nauseating.

"Mr. Tasker, may I tell you something?" Abigail asked.

"Of course you can, Abby." She had asked him to call her that. He thought it might bring back bad memories, but he honored her request. He was also aware that Abigail had a young girl's crush on him. He found it unsettling, but given all she had been through, he felt it was a good sign.

"I feel dirty," she said. "I can't shake this feeling."

"No reason for that, Abby. No reason at all. Listen to me." He looked into her eyes intently, then asked, "Are you listening?"

"Yes."

"Nothing—absolutely nothing—that's happened to you is in any way your fault. You've endured a hell I can't even imagine, but it was inflicted on you by purely evil men. None of it was your doing… and it's over. You will never have to do anything again that you don't want to do. The Pembrooks will see to that. They have enough wealth to give you and

Michael the life you deserve."

"Caleb, I can't get what I've done over the past years out of my mind. I can't sleep. I have nightmares. Will it ever go away?"

"I've done a whole lot of bad things in my life, things I'd be ashamed to tell you, things that would make your young ears ring, even after all you've been through. I can tell you that, with time—maybe a long time—but with time, they fade to a level you can accept. I doubt you'll ever forget the past, but there will come a time when you can handle it. I know that because I know how strong you are. Hell, you wouldn't be here if you weren't one of the strongest women I've ever met. Let me tell you one more thing..."

Abigail's head had slowly come to rest on Tasker's shoulder as he spoke. He stopped talking and looked down at her. She was sound asleep, her breathing a gentle, rhythmic snore. He dared not move and stayed there for the next several hours.

As the train was pulling into the Albuquerque station, Abigail awoke. The Pembrooks and Micky were waiting to greet them. Micky and Abigail embraced each other tightly, both crying. Their embrace lasted for minutes. Few words were exchanged between the siblings, but the platform was filled with pure joy.

The Pembrooks stood nearby, smiling and crying, patiently waiting their turn. At last, Tasker introduced the Pembrokes. Smiles and laughter spread all around. Soon, the Pembrooks were hugging the two children, and everyone had tears in their eyes.

Tasker and Cobb moved apart and out of earshot. They, too, were holding back tears.

Tasker sniffled. "It's not often we see good come from what we do," he said.

"It's not," Cobb replied.

"Feels pretty damn fine."

"It does."

The Pembrooks, Micky, and Abigail finally said goodbye to the two detectives, expressing their gratitude. The farewell between Tasker and Abigail was especially emotional. Tasker, to his surprise, realized he could speak with a woman, even a young one, without fixating on his past experiences with his first love and then with Jasmine. It wasn't a romantic feeling he had toward Abigail—more paternal—but definitely a friendship, and it was truly cathartic. Abigail, on the other hand, saw Tasker as her knight of old, armor and all.

She pulled him aside on the train platform. "Will I see you again?" she asked.

"Of course you will. I'll keep in touch."

"When?"

"I don't know that, Abby. Life goes on. You have so much living to do to make up for the past few years. You'll be too busy to worry about when you'll see me again."

"I doubt that," she said. Her eyes closed, and when they opened, she was crying.

Tasker kissed her on the forehead, turned, and slipped away from the station. Cobb saw him leave, said a quick goodbye, and followed.

When Cobb caught up to Tasker, he was glad to see an unfamiliar smile on Tasker's face as the usually stoic detective cleaned his spectacles.

Cobb joked, "I get tired of asking this, but what's next?"

"First, we go to the ranch, get some rest, then report in. We need a long conversation with Mr. Buford Cartwright. This happy gathering was only half our assignment. Now comes the real challenge."

Cobb looked at his friend with a big grin. He said, "Lead

on, Caleb, lead on."

Tasker and Cobb met Cartwright for lunch at a small, upscale saloon on one of Albuquerque's business district streets. When they arrived, Cartwright had already finished his fourth glass of Burgundy Pinot, an imported French Pinot Noir, his favorite. The detectives ordered beers.

"What have you got for us, Buford?" Tasker asked, hoping his friend was still sober enough to brief them.

"Quite a lot, I think. Let me organize my notes." He shifted his considerable bulk in his chair and shuffled through a pile of papers that, to Tasker, looked anything but organized.

Tasker's worry proved unfounded. It appeared the wine only sharpened Cartwright, who thrived amid office chaos. "Got 'em," he said, looking down at his notes, now arranged in an orderly pile.

"I assumed Wolf would not join you on this trip."

Cobb said, "He's holed up with his love in Serpent's Creek."

"Glad to hear the young lady, Abigail, is thriving in her new home with the Pembrooks."

"Buford?" Tasker asked, bringing Cartwright back into focus.

"Fine, fine. Let's begin with your contact in Chicago. I also assumed that would be your next stop."

Tasker nodded. "Indeed."

"I've arranged for two First-Class train tickets. They'll be waiting for you at the train station. Will you need rail accommodations for your horses?"

"Not this trip. We'll give them a well-earned rest at the ranch," Tasker said.

Cobb interrupted, "Wait a minute. Did I hear you say 'first class'? That's new."

"William is especially interested in this case. I have orders – First Class all the way."

"We can live with that," Tasker said. "Did I mention there's a case of Jameson's Irish Whiskey waiting for you at that hovel you call home?"

"You didn't, but it's about time." Cartwright was grinning from ear to ear.

Cobb asked, "Who is our contact in Chicago?"

"His name's Jimmy O'Connor. One of our best, I'm told."

"He's Pinkerton," Tasker said. "Not a Chicago policeman?"

"That's correct, and for good reason. My information indicates that the Chicago Police Department is as crooked as a barrel of snakes, and the image of those crawly things is one you lads should keep vivid in your minds on this little excursion."

"How bad is it?"

"Local politicians, not coppers, run the entire police department. Everyone out there has their hand in the till. You're gonna have to keep this one close. Only us folks until you get something solid, and maybe even after that."

"That sounds ominous," Cobb said.

"Sorry. Best I can do. O'Connor has a stellar reputation. Honest as 'Ol Abe. He'll help you identify our Chicago culprits if anyone can."

Tasker asked the obvious question, "What are we supposed to do with these culprits if we find them?"

Cartwright paused for a moment, then said, "Of course, you'll pump them for anything on the New York end. My gut tells me this people-selling operation has a big boss in New York. What I know about Chicago is that it's a bunch of tiny fiefdoms, which they call wards. Each one is nearly independent, with its own boss — a snake with many heads. I know our headquarters would be glad if you quietly got rid of them when you find them, but I know we can't do that. We're well outside our usual protocols on this one."

"So?"

"I suggest turning them over to O'Connor with any evidence you find. Let him try to navigate that tangled legal system to prosecute them. I don't envy him trying to find one honest man in that den of thieves, but there it is."

"I take it you'll be working on the New York end while we're in Chicago," Cobb said.

"Right you are. My little network of sources will be nose to the grindstone, so keep in touch."

"We will," Tasker said, "and thanks."

Chapter 17

Introduction to the Windy City

Lunch extended into late that night. The next morning, Tasker and Cobb learned that their train accommodations were in a luxurious Pullman palace car on the Atchison, Topeka & Santa Fe Railway. It was a multi-day trip to Chicago, with service to Dearborn Station in Chicago's South Loop.

The journey was peaceful, but as they traveled further east, they drew many curious stares because of their Western clothing and visible firearms. They eventually moved their Pinkerton badges from their vests to the lapels of their town coats, making them visible to all. The stares tapered off.

As they left Dearborn Station in Chicago, each carrying a carpetbag filled with extra clothes and essentials, Cobb observed, "This is a pretty seedy part of town for a major train station."

"According to some of Buford's notes, which I stole while he was passed out, this is 'the Levee.' The heart of Chicago's gambling and prostitution. A lot of villains walking around here."

"So, I see," Cobb said. "This is the largest place I've ever seen."

Outside the station, they hired a driver and a horse-drawn carriage. "Take us to the Grand Pacific Hotel on Clark Street," Tasker said.

"I bloody know where it is, Mister. Ya don't need ta be tellin' me." The driver was Irish to the bone, from his snap-brimmed cap to his insolent attitude. Tasker leaned forward from his seat and smacked the driver on the back of his head with an open hand. The driver jerked around, ready for a fight, until he saw his passengers in their odd Western clothing and Cobb with the butt of a revolver sticking out from under his coat.

Quick as a startled kitten, he said, "Sorry, mister. Grand Pacific on Clark, comin' right up."

The hotel was unlike anything the Pinkertons had ever encountered. The lobby was a marvel to two Westerners. It radiated wealth and endless luxury, unfamiliar on their frontier. The lobby was a massive room, extravagantly furnished as a central gathering spot for hotel guests. A large skylight bathed the interior in bright sunlight. Multiple spaced-out gas-burner lights suggested that even at night, the grand hall would be brightly lit. The people in the lobby, many wandering about, were dressed to the nines in detailed finery. Therefore, the slouch hats, slightly worn town coats, collarless button-up shirts, and dirty pants tucked into tall, dust-covered boots made the detectives stand out like two ducks in a pond full of majestic swans.

"There's even a telegraph office right here in the lobby," Cobb noted.

"And a special room reserved for ladies only, in case they want privacy," Tasker added.

"You sure we can afford this?"

"I reckon so. Buford made the arrangements."

They explored out of pure wonder, marveling at the sheer opulence of it all.

Tasker suggested, "Let's poke our heads in the bar, maybe have a drink before we go to our room."

"Let's."

Upon entering, Cobb said, "Jesus wept. Will ya look at this?"

It was a stark contrast to the dingy, poorly lit saloons they were used to frequenting. The place was filled with men, all elegantly dressed. They lined the long mahogany bar and sat at the numerous tables. The room was almost as large as the lobby, but the massive chandelier in the center, along with the mirrors behind the bar and on the walls, provided plenty of light. It felt more like a social club than a whiskey saloon. The men at the tables seemed to be conducting business or making deals, not just getting drunk. The absence of 'soiled doves' in provocatively scanty clothing was unmistakable.

"Did you notice, Caleb, there are no working-class stiffs like us in here?"

"I did, and we stand out like two nuns in a brothel, but, hell, this is where Buford arranged for us to meet this O'Connor fella tomorrow at noon."

"I think we might skip that drink. Let's get a good night's sleep," Cobb suggested. "I can't sleep on trains."

"Me neither. I brought my whiskey flask filled with Jameson's, so we don't need to mingle with these dandified fellas until tomorrow."

After seeing the lobby and bar, their room was no surprise. It matched the luxurious décor perfectly, featuring two beds and a private bathroom for morning routines—no need to share facilities down the hall. Tasker and Cobb finished the whiskey flask and collapsed each onto their own beds between silk sheets. Though they complained that the beds were 'too damned soft,' they fell asleep within seconds.

Jimmy O'Connor arrived right on time at noon at the hotel bar. He was about the same height as Tasker, with curly brown hair, dressed in a sharp gray suit, a double-breasted vest, a black cravat with a gold stick pin, and shiny Congress boots. As he approached the table where Tasker and Cobb waited, he removed his stylish bowler hat and looked every bit the part of a banker or even a politician. His clean-shaven face gave him a youthful appearance that belied his age.

O'Connor said, "Guess I don't have to ask if you're Tasker and Cobb. Your garb rather stands out." He was grinning with an affable smile.

"Good observation skills," Tasker said, somewhat sarcastically. Both detectives rose and shook O'Connor's hand, noting his firm grip.

"Will Pinkerton speaks very highly of you both. I'm here to help in your quest wherever I can."

"Guess we do stand out a mite," Cobb said, trying to smooth over Tasker's not-so-subtle first exchange. "The desk clerk suggested we rush off to see a local tailor."

Tasker added, "I explained that it wasn't going to happen."

"Good," O'Connor said. "Screw them. You look fine. What would you like to drink? May I suggest a Sazerac? It's a drink I found in New Orleans. It's made with rye whiskey, bitters, and a dash of absinthe."

"Why not?" Tasker asked, pushing aside the beer he had almost finished. Cobb did the same.

O'Connor called over a waiter and placed an order. They chatted until the drinks arrived.

"Very nice," Tasker said after taking a sip. Cobb nodded in approval.

"So, how can I help?" O'Connor asked.

Cobb said, "We need to understand the lay of the land in the local criminal world, for starters."

Tasker added, "In Socorro, we also picked up a name, Mrs. Zelda Grimm. She allegedly runs things in Chicago, but our source is shaky."

"You could say downright unreliable," Cobb said, thinking of Marv Denton, "but it is a name. He also mentioned the name 'Turpin" as a possible New York contact for the gang, but nothing further."

"I see. I don't recognize either of them, but I'll look into it. I can tell you that you've chosen a good place to start your quest. Allow me to share my background. I'm second-generation Irish, born right here in Chicago. My father, an old-fashioned Irishman if ever there was one, came here by boat, got married, and became a 'copper' on the Chicago Police Department. Dad and my Ma died in the Great Fire back in '71, but I grew up with coppers as part of my family and still have many contacts within the department. I should say straight off the bat that although they may be like my loving family, the vast majority of them are crooked as a dog's hind leg."

"We have our share of bad lawmen out West, so we understand," Cobb said.

"I'm not sure you understand how deep their corruption goes. Chicago is divided into wards, each led by an alderman and a political boss. The police department is split into precincts, each within a ward. To make matters worse, each ward also has a shady gangster boss who gives orders to the political boss.

"The police have a nominal centralized command structure. The precincts operate largely independently within their wards. There is no genuine merit system in the department. The precinct captains answer to politicians who control all police matters, including recruitment, promotions, and, unfortunately, operations. This setup shields top-level criminals. If an officer crosses the line, such as by trying to arrest a protected criminal, he's out—possibly permanently. This understanding keeps other officers in line."

"Impressive," Tasker said.

"Pretty nice setup for the lawbreakers," Cobb said.

"That seems to imply we're really on our own here. No police," Tasker added.

"That's about it, gentlemen," O'Connor said. "I'd like to say it's gonna change down the road, but I seriously doubt it."

"So, how do we proceed?"

"From what I gather, the gang you're after primarily kidnaps poor, parentless boys and girls from the streets, then sells them into slavery or prostitution somewhere out west."

"That's pretty much everything," Cobb said.

"How do they get them to come along?" O'Connor asked.

"They often persuade children to come willingly by pretending it's part of the legitimate child welfare 'placing out' system. Once the children realize their mistake, it's too late. They're then taken the rest of the way by force, like prisoners, and guarded. They use beatings, withholding food, death threats, and torture to keep the children in line. They're scum."

"I think I see why William Pinkerton is so determined to take down this gang of crooks. By the way, after we leave here, he wants to see you."

"That's fine," Tasker said. "He's an old friend."

"Look, what I'll do is send out some feelers. Until recently, I've been working under a false identity within some local unions, gathering information to help the agency avoid strikes. As a result, I have several young, shrewd hoodlums on my payroll. This gang is unusual. There may be rumblings on the street.

"Our worst neighborhood is the 1st Ward, where 'the Levee' is located. You might have seen some of it when you traveled from the train station to this hotel. We are currently in the 1st Ward. I'll start here and see what I can find out without ruffling any gangster's feathers or bringing in the police. Shall we go see William? Our office is within walking distance to the north."

"You haven't changed much," Tasker said as he, Cobb, and O'Connor entered William Pinkerton's imposing office. Pinkerton looked as if he had stepped out of a Carte de Visite—solid build, black suit, double-breasted vest, starched shirt, cravat with a diamond stickpin, and, of course, a thick, imposing mustache. Although the resemblance was there, William did not carry the same solemnity in his face as his father. He had his two beloved Gordon Setters nestled next to a massive desk, on guard.

"A little older, maybe," Pinkerton said. "You look fit, Caleb."

"Clean living and a bottle of fine whiskey a day," Tasker joked. His friendship with William Pinkerton dated back to the war, when the two had seen action together and spied for William's father, Allen Pinkerton. This included when William Pinkerton received a knee wound from an exploding artillery shell at Antietam in 1862. He couldn't walk, and Tasker pulled him out of a dangerous situation.

"Sit down, please. I suppose Jimmy has brought you up to speed."

"He has," Tasker said.

"I also suspect you wonder why my brother Robert and I are so keen on destroying this particular organization of miscreants."

“A little, Will, but it’s not really my business,” Tasker said.

“Nevertheless, I’ll tell you. For years, my father, Robert, and I have invested in what’s known as the ‘Orphan Train Program,’ among other names. Are you familiar with it?”

“I am,” Tasker said. Cobb nodded.

“Good. As you may know, it was started around 1854 by a friend of mine, Charles Price, to relocate poor and homeless children from the crowded Eastern cities to better lives farther west. They were transported west in what later became known as ‘Orphan Trains.’ This remains a worthy cause close to my family’s heart. We have been dedicated financial supporters from the beginning.

“This gang from New York, Chicago, or wherever is an abomination, a blight on the earth. It completely undermines Charles Price’s legitimate efforts to ‘place out’ these poor children and tarnishes my family’s reputation by association. Thank God our father died before seeing this. Robert and I want it stopped, Caleb, and we don’t much care how it’s done as long as it’s legal.”

“Tasker said, “I understand. We will make it happen.”

“I knew we could count on you, Sergeant Major Cobb, and Sammy Wolf-Killer. If anyone can make this happen, it’s the three of you. Be careful, though; we don’t know how big this hornet’s nest is. In any case, you have the full resources of the Agency at your disposal.”

Tasker and Cobb nodded and stood to leave. Pinkerton said, “How’s Sammy doing? I was disappointed he wasn’t with you. My wife has taken a real shine to that boy.”

“He’s fine, Will. He’s about to get hitched, so we call on him only when we need his skills.”

“When you see him, pass along our best.”

“We will.”

Back at the hotel bar, Tasker, who was now much more friendly with O'Connor, said, "We'll wait to hear from you, Jimmy."

"It'll be soon. I'll get on it right away."

When they were alone, Cobb asked, "Do you really think Marv Denton's lead is worth spending too much time on it?"

Tasker replied, "Well, it's a 'grim' lead, but we'll have to wait and see."

Cobb chuckled. "*Pendejo*," he said.

O'Connor returned to them the next day. "Zelda Grimm did the trick. She's known around the 1st Ward. She's a banker with underworld connections. She writes the checks."

"That fits with our information," Tasker said.

"There's more. Interestingly, Zelda is married to a villain named Jake Grimm."

Tasker couldn't help himself, and he was on his fifth beer. "Jake, or Jacob Grimm, he doesn't perchance collect fairytales, does he?"

"Very funny. No, but he's rumored to have his grubby hands in a lot of criminal enterprises out West."

Tasker grew serious. "How do we find the Grimm family?"

"I can take you directly to their lodgings."

"Let's go!" said Tasker, sobering up quickly.

"First, let's head back to your room and do something about those big hog legs you're carrying for everyone to see." O'Connor himself was carrying a small .41 Colt Thunderer revolver in a shoulder holster, out of sight. The trio went up to the hotel room, where Tasker and Cobb took off their gunbelts.

"What now?" Cobb asked.

O'Connor had a briefcase with him. From it, he took two small Smith & Wesson .38 pocket pistols and handed one to each of them. "Put these in your pants or inside coat pockets. They hold five rounds, are single-action, and are fully loaded, so be damned careful. Don't drop 'em."

"Much obliged," Tasker said.

Cobb nodded.

The three left the hotel, and it was a short walk to the tenement house where O'Connor said the Grimms lived. After climbing three flights of rickety stairs, they knocked on the door of a rundown apartment. The door opened to reveal a sturdy, rather good-looking woman slightly taller than Cobb. She was fair-skinned, with curly blond hair, and dressed in a gray day dress. She was polite and asked, "Can I help you?"

To the detectives' surprise, O'Connor pushed his way into the apartment, knocking the woman aside. A man sat in a stuffed chair. He jumped to his feet, ready to run, but there was nowhere to go.

"Hold it, Grimm!" shouted O'Connor, his pistol drawn. "You can't outrun a bullet!"

"You, coppers?"

"What do you think?" O'Connor said. He shoved the man back into the chair. The woman, apparently Mrs. Grimm, was regaining her balance after being pushed aside.

Tasker liked how O'Connor managed things, even if it was surprising. Both detectives quickly understood the situation and responded appropriately, acting as if they were police officers with evidence of a crime.

Tasker said, "We've got checks written by you, Mrs. Zelda Grimm, to folks out West, for taking children into prostitution and slave labor. We also have testimony from some of the children that you, Mr. Grimm, are the boss of this gang of felons, running the whole operation. We're gonna put you away for a long time."

They never dared deny who they were, but Jacob Grimm stayed silent. Zelda, on the other hand, folded like a bad poker hand. "I told you this was a mistake. You and your bullshit ideas. Big man, big boss, yer nothin' but a mistake … my mistake. You think those bigwigs are gonna protect us? I told ya! Now ya got damned cowboys all the way from out West comin' after us. Probably damned savages. We're dead meat, ya fool!"

Jacob Grimm shouted, "Shut your mouth, Zelda, before you get us both killed!" He began to stand from the chair. Cobb slapped him hard across the face, knocking him back into the chair with a thud that nearly tipped it over.

"Leave him alone!" Zelda sniveled, tears streaming down her cheeks. "He may be stupid, but he's my fuckin' stupid."

Tasker thought, *We must look quite menacing to these Easterners.*

O'Connor softly said what Tasker was already thinking: "Nobody's seen us come in here yet, Caleb. Let's not push our luck by taking these two somewhere else. I believe Zelda will tell us everything we need to know right here and now."

"Yup," Tasker whispered back. He pulled Cobb aside to share the strategy. Then he and O'Connor took Zelda to another room in the apartment, out of Jacob's sight and hearing.

O'Connor tied her to a chair. Her eyes and body language showed she was nervous and scared. "What ya gonna do with me?"

O'Connor leaned down to speak into her ear. "Understand me, Zelda," he said in a consoling voice, "If you tell us about this whole ring of reprobates selling children, we might let you and your friend go on your merry way. We don't want you. We want the top dogs. On the other hand, we know a lot about your business. If you leave out one little detail, one morsel of information, I'll have my large friend out there slit Jacob's throat. Then I'll take great pleasure in slitting yours."

O'Connor was right. Zelda was a fountain, overflowing

with information, with occasional prodding.

She told a strange story of intrigue, corruption, and debauchery. "It wasn't us, you understand. I only took care of paying people off, and Jacob only oversaw the movement of the merchandise."

"You mean the children?" O'Connor emphasized the word "children."

"Yes, the children. We never harmed 'em, but some of the others were pretty brutal."

"We know all that, so get on with it. We understand how the business works. Who were the bosses?"

"They'll kill us!"

O'Connor slapped her across the face. "And you think I won't?"

She was sobbing again. "I'll tell ya, ya bastards," she paused to collect herself, "The man who runs it all. The man you'll never even get near is too well protected. He lives above one of those Chinese opium dens somewhere on Clark Street – I don't know exactly. He's guarded by one of those Chinese gangs, tongs, or whatever they call themselves. They're on his payroll, along with other thugs, real bad ones. He never leaves the place, far as I know. He sends his thugs out to do whatever he wants us to do. I've only seen him once at a distance. Jacob pointed him out."

"Name?"

"They call him 'Chinese' Paddy Doyle, but I heard his real name is Cormac Doyle. He's supposed to be one of them who loves to hurt people, a what do you call it…"

"Sadist?" Tasker suggested.

"Yeah, a sadist."

"How many guards does Doyle have in total?" Tasker asked.

I don't know. Jacob tells me twenty or thirty. He's terrified of ‘em. He saw two of the Chinese slice up a young girl, with swords no less, for trying to run away.

“Is this opium den on Clark Street?” Tasker asked.

“Never mind,” O’Connor said. “I know exactly where it is.”

Tasker and O’Connor moved across the room, watching as Zelda struggled with the ropes binding her to the chair.

“You think we can get any more out of her?” Tasker asked.

“No, nor from Jacob,” O’Connor said.

“What’ll we do with these two? I want to kill them, but I guess we can’t do that.”

O’Connor said, “No, but we can sure as hell keep them under wraps until we finish this business. Then it’s my turn to try to find an honest judge in this rotten city. I’ll have my boys take care of these two in the meantime.”

CHAPTER 18

"CHINESE" PADDY DOYLE

Once again, Tasker, Cobb, and O'Connor sat at a table in the hotel bar. Cobb asked O'Connor, "Do you have a plan? This Doyle seems well insulated."

"Of course I do. It's all right here," he said, tapping his head.

"Mind sharing?" Tasker asked.

"We knew Doyle by name. We knew he ran a small prostitution ring here. We didn't realize he was involved in buying and selling humans outside Chicago. He's not far down the criminal pecking order from Michael Cassius McDonald, known as the 'Kingpin' of the 'Windy City.'"

"Who's this McDonald, and why is it called the Windy City?" Tasker asked.

"McDonald is Chicago's top crime boss, involved in everything. He takes a cut if someone breaks wind, as long as there's a profit to be made. However, breaking wind isn't why Chicago earned the nickname 'The Windy City.' It comes from newspapers calling out our crooked politicians for being full of 'hot air.' That's definitely not a compliment. McDonald built the corrupt political machine we're stuck with—damn the bastard. This Doyle character has his own independent gangster ring, but I'd be shocked if McDonald didn't get a share of Doyle's earnings."

This time, it was Cobb asking, "If the police are out of the picture and McDonald protects him, how do we get at him?"

"Interesting question. I've been pondering it myself. I can organize a raid on Doyle's opium den with as many local Pinkertons as we need. No police, only some of our personnel on standby to disrupt local union strikes when necessary. They'd be glad to get a break from those duties. I'm not quite sure that's the right move yet."

"I tend to agree," Tasker said, as he mulled over other possibilities.

"Maybe I can help," Cobb said.

Tasker looked at Jimmy. "Did I mention that our Jefferson Cobb here, former Sergeant Major Cobb of [th]e 10th Cav, educated himself at his master's expense while he was a slave in the South? He knows more about strategy and devious schemes than I do, and I went to West Point."

"I see," said O'Connor.

"Tell us, Sergeant Major," Tasker said.

"I do have an idea," Cobb replied, a hint of mock condescension in his voice. "Somewhere between Sun Tzu and Machiavelli lies a strategic, devious, and, I must say, ruthless solution."

Tasker and O'Connor smiled. Each took a swig of beer and leaned toward the table to catch every word Cobb said.

O'Connor said, "Carry on, Sergeant Major."

Cobb began. "As I see it, our first objective is to destroy Doyle's operation while at the same time learning more about the New York connection. To then destroy it, of course. Is that not so, gentlemen?"

"It is," Tasker said, "although that might be two objectives."

"Given that, our problem is how to do this without stirring up the McDonald faction to interfere or come after us."

"Indeed," O'Connor said.

Cobb waved his hand. "Why not let McDonald's boys take care of all our problems?"

"How?" Tasker and O'Connor asked simultaneously.

Cobb laid out his plan, intricate in its design but entirely feasible. The three agreed to pursue it.

First, they needed to kidnap a few of Doyle's known minions without arousing suspicion about themselves or the Pinkerton Agency. That task was easily handled. O'Connor assigned a couple of his operatives from the Chicago Pinkerton Office to monitor the opium den on Clark Street. They tracked the comings and goings of numerous members of the crime ring and identified two who often strayed too far from their base. With bandanas covering the lower part of their faces, they caught the two hoodlums, one Chinese and one White, at a brothel, half-dressed. The two were knocked out from behind while in the act. Hoods were placed over their heads, and they were quickly taken to a secluded warehouse.

The same tactic was used against McDonald's followers. They kidnapped one of McDonald's workers and hid him away, with a hood over his head, in a second remote warehouse.

"Is this gonna work?" O'Connor asked.

"Looks like it," Tasker said.

"It'll work!" Cobb said with more conviction than he had.

Next, O'Connor identified a brothel and a gambling house under McDonald's direct control. The following night, dressed as local hoodlums to blend in and wearing face coverings, Tasker, Cobb, and O'Connor led about thirty Pinkerton men in raiding both establishments. They quickly entered and exited, taking the night's proceeds from both locations. They left a Chinese Tong member unconscious at the brothel and left Doyle's other man unconscious at the gambling joint.

Before the night ended, the Pinkertons moved to Doyle's opium den headquarters. "I'll go in first. Alone," O'Connor said. "When they open the door, the rest of you ram your way through. You have clubs, not guns, so move fast so you don't get shot or stabbed by some Chinese Tong prick."

O'Connor, with his bandana pulled up, knocked on the metal door. A tall Tong member wearing a big smile opened it. O'Connor hit him over the head with his club and rushed past, followed by about thirty Pinkertons with their faces covered.

"Get to it, boys," he said. Sleepy, dazed patrons of the opium den were lurching about, trying to get out.

Doyle barricaded himself in his second-floor office. O'Connor, Tasker, and Cobb stood on each side of the door.

O'Connor shouted, "Open up, Doyle. We've got a little message for you from McDonald."

Two quick shots came through the door, narrowly missing Tasker.

O'Connor reached into his coat and pulled out a cylindrical object with a short fuse attached to one end. He motioned for Tasker and Cobb to step back down the stairs, lit the fuse, placed the object next to the door, and then ran back down to join the detectives on the stairs.

A loud, jarring blast was followed by a cloud of smoke filling the hallway.

Tasker whispered to Cobb, "I do so like O'Connor's style."

Cobb agreed. "No talk, all action."

Led by O'Connor, the three pushed through the smoke to find the door off its hinges and blown into Doyle's office. Doyle had apparently heard the fuse burning and was cowering behind his desk, dazed and in shock.

As it turned out, only about a dozen Chinese Tong members and half a dozen local henchmen were present in the opium den. The Pinkertons tore through the place, including Doyle's office, furniture, wallpaper, and curtains – everything was wrecked. They hooded Doyle before he could see any of them and took him to the Pinkerton Office without speaking to him, despite his protests.

He had no idea who they were or where he was being held, but he wasn't happy. He warned them repeatedly through the hood covering his head, "Yer dead men! Yer all fuckin' dead men! I'll find ya and kill every one of ya!"

Tasker commented, "Feisty, isn't he?"

"He is," Cobb said.

O'Connor told Tasker and Cobb, "You gentlemen go back to the hotel. I need some time alone with Mr. Doyle."

Tasker hesitated to leave this delicate interrogation in O'Connor's hands alone, but Cobb said, "Let it be, Caleb. Jimmy's on his own stomping grounds. Let's trust him."

A few hours later, O'Connor found Tasker and Cobb at their usual table in the hotel bar.

"Where's Doyle?" Tasker asked, assuming he was probably dead.

"On ice for now," was all O'Connor said, but he added, "I have more information, though. Doyle confirmed the New York name you gave me, Turpin. I checked, and his full name is Adam Turpin. He's a businessman in New York City, in the firearms business—buying and selling. He's Doyle's boss, though Doyle handles the Chicago side of the human marketing operation entirely. Turpin lives at Number

5, Gramercy Park, an upscale residential neighborhood in the city. Sounds like big money.

"My boys did well raiding McDonald's brothel and gambling house. As you saw, they wrecked everything, stole the proceeds, and left Doyle's unconscious hoodlums, one in each place. They also did well at Doyle's headquarters, completely destroying the opium den and Doyle's office, leaving McDonald's boy behind. This worked flawlessly, Jefferson. They're at each other's throats. It was a brilliant plan."

Cobb blushed. "Glad it worked. Never had a doubt." He laughed.

O'Connor continued, "I'll send Doyle to one of McDonald's enterprises, all wrapped up like a Christmas present, sometime tomorrow. McDonald already has the evidence that Doyle raided him, but there'll be a lot of teeth-gnashing and maybe a killing or two over who's to blame, all to Chicago's benefit. McDonald still has his organization intact, but if he doesn't kill Doyle—which is highly unlikely—I'll see about prosecuting the bastard somewhere. Hell, McDonald might even help with that. I'll keep you informed."

Cobb asked, "I'm curious. How'd you get so much information so fast from Doyle?"

"I have a method I've used before to get information from unwilling suspects. You tie their ankles to heavy weights and secure their arms behind their backs. Then you take them to a dock on the Chicago River and dangle the weights and their lower legs over the edge. They understand quickly and usually become very cooperative afterward. Sometimes, even the threat of doing it makes tough men sing like a bluebird. Anyway, it worked on Doyle, although I doubt he'd ever admit it."

"You're a very unusual man, Jimmy O'Connor," Cobb said. "Remind me to stay your friend."

"We shall always be so, Sergeant Major Jefferson Cobb," he said.

Tasker raised a toast. "The Chicago ring of child sellers is no more. New York is next."

"Best of luck, my friends."

Chapter 19

New York City

Tasker and Cobb, their Western attire still sharply contrasting with how big-city folks dressed, arrived at Grand Central Terminal in New York City, exhausted from the long train ride. It was a massive, open building filled with travelers, but that wasn't the surprising part. They had come from Chicago, another bustling metropolis and the largest place the two detectives had ever seen. Even inside the terminal, the difference was noticeable. The crowd was thicker and more frenzied. This became the norm, not the exception, when comparing Chicago and New York.

They left the terminal, rented a Hansom cab, and headed to the Fifth Avenue Hotel, where Cartwright had booked a room. The busy streets made Chicago seem quiet by comparison as the horse-drawn cab navigated crowded avenues from one traffic jam to the next. The buildings looked closer together and taller than in the Windy City.

The hotel was very similar to their accommodations in Chicago—overly luxurious, in the eyes of the two Westerners. The sharply dressed clerk behind the hotel counter looked at them with one eyebrow raised, clearly showing disdain as he asked, "Gentlemen, are you sure you have the right hotel?"

As he spoke, two burly men in frock coats, starched shirts, and cravats, still looking like thugs, moved behind the detectives. The bulges under their coats indicated they were armed. Cobb's shotgun and Tasker's Winchester were in soft leather, Indian-beaded cases, and their Colts were in their carpet bags. However, they still carried the small pocket pistols O'Connor had kindly given them in their inside coat pockets.

Tasker and Cobb still hadn't answered the hotel clerk's question, and the tension in the air was mounting. The clerk pressed on, "There are, I'm sure, more suitable accommodations down toward the Five Points. We also have a standing policy about Negroes." He looked at Cobb, and his raised eyebrow seemed to rise even higher. One of the thugs behind the detectives muttered under his breath, "Uppity Nigger."

Tasker and Cobb were about to explain to the clerk and the two thugs their thoughts on the hotel rules and the clerk's condescending attitude when about five or six tall, well-dressed men appeared out of nowhere and surrounded the thugs. The tallest, a handsome gentleman dressed to the nines, said, "Gentlemen, gentlemen. Let's slow down."

The clerk blurted out, "Mr. Colonna, how grand to see you. Can I help you, sir?"

"These two gentlemen are with me. By the way, they are close friends of Mr. Pinkerton and, in fact, are Pinkerton Agents themselves, two of our most prestigious detectives."

"I had no idea," the astonished and humbled clerk said.

"You will give them one of your very best rooms, I believe, under Mr. Cartwright's name."

"Of course, Mr. Colonna, of course." He hustled to hand them a key.

"Room 225, second floor," he said. The two thugs looked confused.

Colonna asked the detectives, "Can I show you to the bar for a drink? The page will take your bags."

Thus far, Tasker and Cobb had said very little, somewhat amused by the whole affair. They were used to being a little more direct in their approach. Tasker said, "Don't mind if we do, a drink would be welcome, but there's one more little thing."

As they turned away from the clerk's desk, they looked at each other and nodded. Tasker delivered a firm blow to one thug's jaw. Cobb punched the other in the stomach with his left hand, then, as the man bent over, struck him on the top of the head with his right, landing a thundering, jaw-wrenching blow. Both thugs collapsed to the floor. Tasker's thug was bleeding and half-conscious. Cobb's thug was knocked out. The clerk was in shock.

Colonna burst into laughter, as did the Pinkerton men with him. Tasker and Cobb reached into the thugs' coats, drew their pistols, and emptied the chambers. The sound of cartridges rattling on the floor echoed through the hotel lobby, drawing patrons' attention. Cobb placed both guns on the startled clerk's desk and said, "You should be careful of these. They could hurt someone." The clerk let out a small squeak of recognition.

Like Chicago, the opulent bar was very masculine, though upper-class women might visit the hotel's public lounges and dining rooms. Men came here to socialize, network, and conduct discreet business while enjoying the latest exotic drinks. Colonna, Tasker, and Cobb sat at one table, while Colonna's other Pinkertons sat at another.

"I'm Lorenzo Colonna, gentlemen. The boss has assigned me as your contact while you're here."

"Pleased to meet you," Tasker said. "I'm Caleb Tasker."

"Likewise," Cobb added, "I'm Jefferson Cobb."

"Tell me why you're here, gentlemen, though I think I already know most of it."

"We're on the trail of a jasper named Adam Turpin. Know him?"

"Can't say I do, but it's a big city, and crime is rampant."

"Turpin is a somewhat sophisticated criminal by our Western standards. He's organized a sinister ring that sells children off the streets of New York into slave labor and prostitution as far out as the territories."

"Cobb added, "He had folks in Chicago helping in the same business from out there, but I think we broke their backs pretty much before we came here. We know he's still operating in your city."

Colonna said, "I take it he's sending them west by train. It strikes me he'd have to be well connected to the railroads somehow." He pushed his hand through his thick, black hair. "And maybe he has serious political clout. We need to be vigilant."

"I've got to tell you," Cobb interrupted, "I spent years down south and out west in the cavalry, and this all feels pretty new to me. I guess I've gotten used to the wide-open spaces and the rough justice we chase out there. Chicago was bad enough, but it looks like New York's even worse. The noise, the crowds, and the anonymity of this city kind of overwhelm me."

"You'll get used to it soon enough," Colonna said. "How about you, Caleb?"

"I grew up in Pennsylvania, attended West Point, and spent much of the war in the East. I must admit, though, this is one big city."

They began their New York work by meeting Robert Pinkerton at his Manhattan office. It was similar to the meeting with William, except that Tasker didn't know Robert as well as he knew William. Still, Robert assured him of his office's full support in stopping this threat to children. Robert officially appointed his second-in-command, Lorenzo Colonna, to work with Tasker and Cobb.

As they were leaving the meeting, Robert gave them a sincere warning: "Be careful of the police; they're not as bad as those in my brother's beloved Chicago, but be careful. That's why you have Lorenzo. Count on him. Most police officers here are of Irish, Italian, or German descent, with the Irish making up the majority. Tammany Hall, the political machine that runs New York, is also largely Irish. Lorenzo has trustworthy contacts who are not Irish. Good luck."

When they returned to the hotel bar, Tasker asked Colonna, "Tell us about this Tammany Hall."

Colonna explained, "Tammany Hall is the Democratic Party's political machine. Unlike Chicago, which is divided into semi-independent wards, New York's machine is centralized under what is referred to as Tammany Hall.

"They have very close ties to organized crime —I mean very close — and their influence on city affairs is unbreakable. This includes the police. There's widespread patronage and a large bloc of immigrant voters that keep them in power. Their relationship with organized crime creates a network of protection, graft, and political favoritism that has a stranglehold on the city."

"It definitely sounds like Chicago," Tasker said, "maybe on a larger scale with a more robust and efficient chain of command."

Cobb asked, "What's the best way to move?"

"We try the chain of command first," Colonna said.

"If we know they're crooked, why do that?" Cobb asked.

"To protect ourselves. If we go through the back door first, and the high command or politicians find out, they can shut us down quickly, claiming we didn't follow proper protocol. I want to use my contacts in law enforcement, but I also want to ensure their safety. If we hit a dead end going the upfront way, which we probably will, then my contacts can help us move forward under the cover of following up on leads to shut the case down completely."

"I guess you know what you're doing," Cobb said, though he was not entirely convinced, nor was Tasker.

Colonna went straight to a precinct captain and presented the evidence against Adam Turpin. The captain took notes on the evidence but remained noncommittal. Later that day, Colonna was informed that Case Number 88-10101 had been assigned and that the case would be handed over to the detectives. A week later, Colonna learned from his sources in the department that the case had been dismissed, meaning it had been filed under *"Insufficient Evidence/Not Cost-Effective to Pursue*."

Colonna called a meeting with Tasker and Cobb. "As I suspected, the word about the evidence reached Tammany Hall at some level, and the case was shut down. Now I can move through my contacts within the department, and at least have a case number to cover their activities should we need it. If the matter had originated within the department rather than from an outside source, such as the Pinkerton Agency, it still would have been dismissed. However, the officers who brought it up would likely have been reprimanded or transferred to the far reaches of Long Island, where they would direct traffic or issue tickets for minor offenses.

"Good," said Tasker. "We understand. So, now what?" Their tone showed they had grown impatient with waiting around in their luxurious hotel and were drinking way too much.

"Oh, ye of little faith. The good news is that here in New

York, we still have a few honest coppers and politicians. The even better news for you is that I know most of them. In fact, someone will meet us at a safe location outside the city tonight. He's a sergeant in the New York Police Department. Also, a well-known politician, New York Senator Roger Anthony Swane, has agreed to help us and provide some political cover."

"How do we know either of these jaspers can be trusted?" Cobb asked, always suspicious.

"The copper's name is Nickola Antonelli. Does that sound very Irish to you?" Colonna asked.

"No."

"We've been friends since childhood. We're from the same village in Italy, Sonnino, near Rome. There are several more coppers on the force we trust, from the same village or nearby."

"Aren't there Italian criminals, or are they all Irish?" Cobb asked, dripping with sarcasm.

Colonna allowed the jab to fade away unchallenged. He said, "For sure, but we Italians know our gangsters and how to handle them, and they're small potatoes. Not nearly as widespread or dominant as the Irish. Maybe in years to come because they're growing, but not now."

"How do your honest Italian officers survive in such a twisted world?" Tasker asked.

"They have their ways, but mostly they keep their heads down as much as possible. They toe the line as far as their conscience allows, but they would never, never, ever go against 'family,' and being from the same village or region is considered 'family' by us Italians."

"What about the politician?" Cobb asked.

"One of the loudest voices in politics opposing political corruption, and especially police corruption. I trust him."

Colonna went to relieve himself, giving Tasker and Cobb a chance to talk.

"I trust Colonna because Pinkerton trusts him, but what about this copper and the politician?" Cobb said.

"I don't think we have many options, Jefferson. This is their territory, and we either trust someone or head home with our tails between our legs. You agree?"

"I do, but I'm still holding on to this pocket pistol."

Colonna bundled them into a Hansom cab. They moved cautiously through the ever-darkening streets to a tenement house on the edge of the notorious Five Points, in what was called 'Little Italy.'

In a dingy room on the second floor, they were introduced to a dark-complexioned man wearing a town coat and a high derby. His long black hair, sticking out from under the derby, was complemented by a thin mustache and a small tuft of hair beneath his lip.

Colonna made the introductions. "This is Sergeant Nickola Antonelli, New York Police Detective. He likes to be called Nick." They greeted each other and shook hands all around.

Tasker explained their mission to Antonelli. His reaction was similar to Colonna's, but it felt more personal. "I get the picture. Scum of the earth, preying on children. Scum of the earth. I'll be proud to help you get 'em, and I've got some friends on the force who will be happy to join us."

Colonna updated Antonelli on his progress, including Case Number 88-10101. "That's good. We can leverage that." The police detective paused. "May I make a suggestion?"

"Of course," said Tasker. "That's what we're hoping for. This town isn't like the prairies we're used to, and in Chicago, we couldn't go to the police. This is a welcome change."

"Yeah," Antonelli said. "There are still a few of us who

haven't been fully corrupted."

"Let me pair you with two patrolmen I trust. They can guide you to some of our orphanages and shelters. You're looking for any pattern of children disappearing that might point to Turpin's insidious little network."

"That sounds like a start," Tasker said.

"Meanwhile, I'll send some detectives to poke around the railroad yards and talk to employees. Maybe we can find out more about how they're using the railroads to transport these children west. My guess is that some railroad officials are up to their necks in this business."

Tasker was teamed with Antonio Caetani, a senior patrolman, and Cobb with a patrolman named 'Big John' Callisto. They were complete opposites in appearance. Caetani was small and bristly, about five feet six inches tall, while Callisto was a giant, as his nickname suggested, well over six feet. They had been friends since birth and could read each other's moves before they made them. Although Caetani was tiny by comparison, he was a champion boxer within the police department and could easily hold his own against men twice his size.

Even working alongside these experienced police officers, the Pinkertons viewed the city itself as an enemy. The maze of streets and alleys in Five Points offered perfect cover for criminal activity in lower Manhattan. Tasker and Cobb were out of their element, driven by a sense of frontier justice and a fierce determination to save innocent children. They prepared to confront an adversary who operated with calculated efficiency right under the noses of ordinary society.

Chapter 20

The Trail Leads West

"I had my doubts," Cobb said after a long day of trudging around Five Points, "but this seems to be working out. Callisto and Caetani, our tall and short of it, really know their business."

"It does, and they do," Tasker said, smiling at Cobb's comical reference to their two police guides to the big city.

Cobb and Callisto, during their travels in the criminal underworld, recruited a former subordinate of Turpin named 'Jippy One-Shoe.' He earned his nickname because a careless surgeon cut off his left foot on the operating table after the Battle of Gettysburg. Since then, he has moved around on crutches and only needs a right shoe. Jippy was angry at his former boss, Turpin, for shortchanging him on payment for his services. He didn't tell the police exactly what those services were. He turned out to be the perfect informant.

Jippy provided them with clues about the identity and home address of one of Turpin's underbosses, Shamus McFadden. According to Jippy, McFadden oversaw the methods and routes used to transport the abducted children. *Just the man we need*, thought Cobb.

Tasker and Caetani, through numerous interviews, identified several railroad workers who helped facilitate the Turpin operation in the New York City railroad yards. Gradually, the team unraveled the criminal enterprise, getting closer to Turpin's boss with each passing day.

In darkness and with the assurance that Senator Swane had them covered, Antonelli led a team of patrolmen to McFadden's residence. They had a warrant for his arrest, and a search warrant for the residence. Unfortunately, he was not there. However, the search uncovered a treasure trove of incriminating documents – client lists, payment invoices, forged travel manifests, and record books detailing bribes to railroad officials. All of this evidence pointed to the meticulous planning needed to move the gang's human cargo out west unnoticed. Turpin's name appeared in nearly every document.

With the overwhelming evidence collected, even the corrupt Tammany Hall politicians couldn't shield Turpin. Colonna and Antonelli brought Tasker and Cobb to meet Senator Swane at his well-appointed 6th Avenue office. To their surprise, he was a youngish, athletic-looking politician about as tall as Cobb, impeccably dressed, and had a full beard. *No doubt to appear older*, thought Tasker. *Politicians make my skin crawl.*

Senator Swane welcomed them to his office, a five-room space with no fewer than three secretaries and an aide.

"Well, gentlemen, it's a pleasure to finally meet you. New York's finest have already sung your praises."

Tasker shook hands. "It's our pleasure, Senator. You've been a great help to our mission."

Cobb also shook his hand and said, "You have, indeed, and thank you."

The Senator lit a cigar and offered one to his guests from a silver box on his large desk. They declined, except for Antonelli, who took one, lit it, and inhaled, satisfied.

"I'm curious," the Senator said. "Might I take a closer look at one of your sidearms?" He addressed Tasker and Cobb, both wearing their Western attire and visibly carrying their Colt revolvers.

"Certainly," Tasker said. He drew his Colt as quickly as a rattlesnake strikes, startling the Senator. Tasker flipped it effortlessly in reverse and handed it over, butt-first.

"My, my, this is heavier than I expected."

"Careful," Tasker warned. "It's loaded."

"I don't doubt it. Have you identified any of Turpin's criminal associates?" He still held the gun, feeling its weight.

Colonna said, "Yes, Senator, the police will be arresting them as soon as Turpin is in custody."

The Senator handed the Colt back to Tasker, holding the barrel awkwardly. "I'd like to see the evidence, if I may," he said.

The evidence presented to the Senator seemed to impress him. "You gentlemen have done this city, and maybe even further, a great service. I congratulate you. Rest assured, I will see to it that warrants for his arrest and a search of his home are immediately issued for Mr. Adam Turpin."

The meeting lasted short of an hour. Enough time for Colonna to have a second cigar. Outside on the street, Colonna asked Tasker, "So, what do you think of the Senator?

"He's a politician. In my experience, they're all alike. The word 'swarmy' comes to mind." He exchanged a knowing look with Cobb.

"He's been a big help to the few friends we have in the police and us," Colonna said.

"Maybe I'll change my view… and maybe not," Tasker

said, ending the discussion.

Because Turpin lived outside the city proper, it took an entire day to process the arrest and search warrants for him and his mansion. A full squad of Antonelli's special team, bells jingling, was transported in a horse-drawn "paddy wagon' to the Turpin mansion in Staatsburg, New York. They were joined by a squad from the Dutchess County Sheriff's Office, which had primary jurisdiction in Staatsburg.

Their knock on the large mahogany doors was answered by a butler, who told them, "Mr. Turpin is not on the premises." Disappointed, the police officers and sheriff's deputies handed the butler the search warrant for the house. He accepted it, but not willingly.

The search was thorough. It uncovered many more documents similar to those found at McFadden's house. Additionally, they found more lists of contacts, presumably recipients of the enslaved children, in multiple locations across the Western states and territories. These lists revealed that the operation was much larger and more widespread than Tasker or Cobb had suspected. The lists included numerous names and payment details, which the Pinkerton detectives could pass on to the U.S. Marshals or local law enforcement for further action.

There was no sign of Turpin. Days later, Calisto's informant, Jippy One-Shoe, told him that Turpin had paid a railroad contact to secure a ticket west. Their pursuit was immediate; they boarded the next available westbound train, carrying enough vital evidence to put Turpin away for decades.

"At least we had a chance to say goodbye to our Italian friends," Cobb said as the steady clatter of the train's wheels kept reminding them of how far ahead their quarry was.

"He was warned," Cobb said.

"He was," Tasker replied.

"Incidentally," Cobb said. "Antonelli gave me this." He pulled a Carte de Visite from his coat pocket and handed it to Tasker. "He identified it as a likeness of Turpin. One of Antonelli's men found it while searching the mansion. Could come in handy."

The man in the image was tall and proud, standing next to a pillar with one hand on his frock coat lapel and the other resting on the pillar. His eyes were sharp, and that was the first thing Tasker noticed. He wore a top hat and looked very much like a New York tycoon.

Tasker handed the image back to Cobb. "You know, Jefferson, we basically accomplished the assignment. We found and returned Abigail, and the gang that took her no longer exists. At least for now, many children are safe from harm."

"We did, didn't we?" Cobb replied, smiling, as he put the image back in his pocket. "Damn shame Turpin got away, but we'll get 'em."

"We will. We'll find Turpin, and he'll lead us to his boss. Not for a second do I believe Turpin is behind all this."

Cobb nodded in agreement.

They spent their time examining maps and evidence, searching for a clue to where Turpin might hide. As they moved west, they felt a sense of freedom, leaving behind a crowded, dirty place for the open spaces where they truly belonged.

Cobb mused, "I never realized how much clean, fresh air meant to me."

Tasker said, "Let's not do that again for a very long time."

"What's that?"

"Go east."

Cobb nodded.

First on their list when they finally reached Albuquerque

was to visit their horses, Blaze and Two-Socks, at the ranch. The house looked good, and the horses were well cared for. The two horses were happy to see Tasker and Cobb, who brushed them down and took them for a long ride. After that, they could focus on themselves. A long bath was in order, along with a change of clothes.

They decided to ride to the Pinkerton Headquarters to give Blaze and Two-Socks more exercise. When they reported in, they were told to see Cartwright first thing.

"You gentlemen have had a busy time. How was the ranch?" Cartwright asked.

"Ranch is fine. I'm damn glad we bought it," Cobb said, thinking how good the fresh clothes felt.

Tasker said, "Manuel did a good job of watching over it while we were away."

"Sorry about Turpin, but the boss is thrilled with the results overall. Mission accomplished."

"About Turpin," Tasker said. "We're fixin' to get him. We figure he might be lying low for a while, but he'll pop up sooner or later."

"Good news, then! He's already popped. My source in Fort Smith says he came through there, hell-bent for leather. Apparently, he was spreading money around, looking to recruit cutthroats for some unspecified perverse enterprise. Maybe restarting his old one."

"Is he still there?" Cobb asked.

"No. He recruited a half-dozen shooters and left with a well-supplied wagon heading west into Indian Territory."

"We'll leave right now. Take the horses with us this time," Tasker said.

"Not so fast," Cartwright said. "I have orders for you both. The boss wants you to take at least two days' rest right here, then you can go after this culprit."

"What?" said Tasker. "We've been resting all the way out here on the damned train. We need to get moving while the trail is still hot."

"All I can tell you is what he said, but I wouldn't cross him. In the meantime, I'll arrange your train tickets to Fort Smith. I'll even set up a stock car for your horses, buy you a pack mule with all the trimmings, and gather enough provisions for several days on the trail after you head out from Fort Smith. That'll take me a day or so. You can thank me later. Incidentally, that case of Jamesons is almost gone. Did I mention you'll be traveling First-Class again?"

Tasker gave up. "Shit, you make the offer too tempting to refuse, and I get the message about the Jamesons." Cobb smiled and shook his head.

On the morning of the third day, Tasker and Cobb arrived at the eight-year-old Albuquerque Train Depot with First-Class tickets to Fort Smith, Arkansas. The route required one transfer because there was no direct railway line. The first leg was on the Atchison, Topeka & Santa Fe Railway to Wichita, Kansas. For this part of the journey, they were booked into a Pullman sleeping car with beds. In Wichita, they would transfer the horses, the mule, and the goods to a livestock car on the Frisco Line. This final leg ran through Indian Territory to Fort Smith. They would ride in a comfortable First-Class passenger car. The whole trip would last four or five days, unless delayed by weather or mechanical issues.

Blaze, Two-Socks, and the newly purchased mule were safely in the stock car, along with their supplies. Cartwright had done a brilliant job. While waiting, Tasker sent a telegram to Sammy Wolf, asking him to meet them in Fort Smith with Wind-in-His-Hair, his beloved roan-colored Mustang. The reply came quickly. It read: *I will be there – Wolf.*

After a day and night on the rails, Tasker leaned back in

his cushioned chair and said, "I am truly getting used to this. It's dangerous." The train's rhythmic wheels were hypnotic.

Cobb said, "It gives you too much time to think."

"What are you thinking about now, Jefferson?"

"Thinking about Abigail, my Abigail."

Tasker nodded. "Funny, I was thinking about Sarah and Jasmine…"

"Women should keep away from us. We're bad luck."

"Spect so," Tasker said, and he fell into a deep sleep.

They switched trains in Wichita without trouble. Horses and gear were transferred to another stock car on the new train. Tasker and Cobb found their seats in a luxury coach car. There were about ten other passengers in their car, the only passenger car on the train.

A woman sitting across from them asked Tasker, "Excuse me, sir, but do you think we'll have any trouble with those heathen savages I've heard so much about?" Her husband, seated next to her in the window seat, leaned forward to hear Tasker's reply.

"I reckon not, ma'am," Tasker said, his face showing no emotion. "Them 'heathen savages' are probably too busy eating their own children."

Cobb laughed out loud.

The woman said, "Humph," and turned away from Tasker.

The husband, to show he was manly, said, "You, sir, are rude." Tasker gave the man the infamous 'look' that Cobb knew well.

The man's eyes looked as if they were bulging from his head, and he kept fidgeting in his seat. He turned to his wife and said, "Never mind, dearest."

With the incessant echo of the train wheels, both detectives soon fell asleep, even Cobb, who rarely, if ever, slept on trains.

It was many hours later when Tasker woke to the sound of gunfire, rubbing his eyes. Cobb was already awake. "Caleb, I think you're gonna have to apologize to that woman."

"Huh?"

"Look out the window."

It was daylight, and about twenty or thirty Indians, dressed in everything from makeshift cowboy clothes and slouch hats to feathered war bonnets, were riding alongside the moving train. They were firing Winchesters, not arrows, at the passenger car. Glass shattered all around them, and the woman and the man across the aisle were both screaming.

To Tasker, they looked much like the Comancheros he remembered from years ago, but he knew better. These were more likely mixed tribe renegades pushed off their land by the government. Their leader, a tall Indian on a striking white horse, reminded Tasker and Cobb of their fight with the Comancheros years earlier, in which Marshal Waylon Sweet was killed.

"It sure looks like him," Cobb said. Tasker knew exactly what Cobb meant.

"It does. Do you want him, or should I?" Tasker asked.

"Your Winchester should do it. My shotgun won't reach."

"What are you doing?" cried the man across the aisle. By this time, the other passengers were in full panic.

Tasker, aiming his rifle, said, "Well, I thought I'd pick off the white horse Jasper out there. Might discourage the others if their leader falls." He let the lead fly and hit the Indian below his war bonnet in the left temple. It threw him off his horse, and he was immediately trampled by the Indians riding behind him.

"That did it," Cobb said. "Look at 'em run off." The Indians were indeed veering off and riding away.

The woman across the aisle said in a loud voice, "You see! Savages! You portrayed them as innocents. I expect an apology."

Her husband said, "Yes, apologize to my wife." They were both standing.

Tasker remained silent, ignoring the couple. Cobb had been sitting through the entire episode. Now Cobb stood up, facing the couple. He said, "Sit down, now!" They did.

He continued, "Those Indians were wrong to attack the train, but they didn't do it without reason. My guess is they were recently torn from the very homes the government gave them in the first place. There's a lot of that going on around here lately. Caleb, here, shot their leader, and they ran off. It would have cost many more lives if he hadn't. He probably saved both your scalps. Now, I suggest you sit quietly and count your blessings for the rest of this trip. Is that clear?"

They both nodded. After all, this huge man who was telling them also held a 12-gauge shotgun.

Cobb sat back down. Tasker leaned into him and whispered, "My, my, we are testy today."

Cobb replied, "Look who's talking."

They slept through the rest of the journey. There wasn't a peep from the couple across the aisle.

CHAPTER 21

FORT SMITH

Like many other Western towns where the railroad passed through, Fort Smith, Arkansas, grew quickly. However, its main claim to fame was not its rapid growth, its businesses, its ranches, or its farming. It was best known as a hub for federal law enforcement. The town was one of the few with permanent gallows for multiple executions. The impressive Federal Courthouse, which included a new jail, housed Judge Isaac Parker's court. Known as 'the hanging judge,' he lived up to that nickname. His Deputy Marshals patrolled not only Arkansas but also the rugged and barren Indian Territory, notorious for outlaw gangs and desperados.

Upon arriving in Fort Smith, Tasker and Cobb retrieved their horses and the mule. They took some time to groom all three after the long journey. The horses, having been confined in the stock car for days, were eager to see them. The mule seemed only glad to get off the train. The detectives then went to the San Sebastian Hotel on Garrison Street, where Cartwright had reserved a room for them. They put Blaze and Two-Socks in the hotel stable.

Sammy Wolf was waiting for them, having been in town for

a full day. Their pattern of arriving in new towns was becoming routine, but the accommodations were gradually losing their appeal. This hotel was about as good as Fort Smith had to offer and featured a decent saloon.

Their first stop was the Federal Courthouse. There was no need to see the judge, but Cobb wanted to find an old friend, Deputy U.S. Marshal Bass Reeves. He and Tasker had met Reeves during a prior assignment in the Territories and Texas involving a murdering outlaw named Morgan Fisk. Reeves and a detail of the 10th Cavalry had helped the Pinkerton detectives gain the upper hand on Fisk in an outlaw-filled town in Texas. This was the case in which Indians had murdered Marshal Sweet, a friend of the two detectives. Later, Fisk killed Sarah, the woman Tasker loved. He shot her and threw the body from a moving train.

Asking for Reeves, they were led to the newly built jail. As they walked through, Wolf was surprised and signed, *"The cells look quite comfortable."*

Cobb said, "Not if yer facing a short rope and a long fall, Snip."

"I suppose not."

They found Reeves sound asleep on a cot in one of the jail cells, his hat covering his face. His hands were crossed peacefully on his chest, and his Deputy U.S. Marshal badge was clearly visible. Cobb knew it was Reeves. There were no other Colored marshals.

"Is that you, Bass?" Cobb asked, knowing the answer.

"That be me, and I know that voice. Howdy, Jefferson." He pulled his hat up as he sat on the edge of the cot. "You a rich man yet?"

"Rich man?"

"I figured with all that private detective money rollin' in, you'd be well set up and retired by now."

"You'd be wrong, old friend. Still only me, Caleb, and Sammy. We're merely plodding along, looking for nefarious evildoers."

"Glad to see all of you. How you doin'?" Reeves said, seeing Tasker and Wolf standing behind Cobb.

"We're doin' fine, Bass," Tasker said. "Good to see you again."

"How about you, Sammy Wolf-Killer?"

Wolf nodded and smiled, then signed, *"I dropped the 'killer' part, Bass. It scared too many folks."*

"Why are you here, Jefferson?"

"Tracking down another villain. A really bad one this time," Cobb explained to Reeves about the child-selling ring, Abigail, and their progress so far in their pursuit of Turpin.

"Children! What's this world comin' to? I heard that name, Turpin, just recently, by God. Yeah, he tried to recruit one of my sniffers. This sniffer is a thief and part-time gun for hire. Uses the name Weasel. I got him off a minor charge a while back, and he's been providing me with some information since then. Mostly useless. He ain't all that reliable. I've filed away most of what he's told me in the past, but recently some of it has begun to make more sense."

Tasker and Cobb pulled up stools in the cell and listened. Wolf remained standing. Reeves continued, "You familiar with the Purdy gang?"

"No," said Tasker. Cobb shook his head.

"Aaron Purdy's the leader. It's quite a large operation, I hear, with maybe twenty members. They work across the Indian Territories but have recently been seen along Snake Creek in Chickasaw country, possibly running illegal whiskey stills. Don't be fooled by the small-time whiskey crimes. They're train robbers and horse thieves, wanted for several murders.

"So, Weasel tells me this joker, Turpin, wanted him to join

a gang he was pulling together. Didn't say why, but Weasel figured it was for nothin' good. Weasel flat turned him down. So did many other local ne'er-do-wells. They didn't trust this Johnny-come-lately Eastern dude. Weasel said he was headin' fer the Snake to get more men. I'm puttin' two and two together and figurin' Turpin might be tryin' to join up with Purdy."

"That supports what we alreadyheard. A Pinkerton source reported that he left Fort Smith with a small group of men heading west," Tasker said.

"You know the country out that way? It's rough, and the Indians don't take to anyone but other Indians, and only those from their own tribe," Reeves said. "As I said, it's mostly Chickasaw Nation territory."

"I don't know that country at all," Tasker said. "You, Jefferson?"

"No."

Wolf shook his head from side to side and signed, *"I don't speak Chickasaw, either."*

Reeves was thinking. "Maybe I can help," he said. "Heck Thomas is out that way, in Whitebead Hill, near Pauls Valley. He's also a Deputy U.S. Marshal under Judge Parker, like me. He went out there and set up an office at the request of the Chickasaw folks. They seem to like him and tolerate his being a non-Indian."

"I've heard the name," Tasker said.

"He's one of the best, next to me, of course," Reeves added.

"That's what I heard," Tasker said, smiling.

"I'll write you one of them letters of introduction … Well, I won't actually write it … still can't." He laughed. "I'll get Judge Parker to do it. The Purdy Gang has been a thorn in Heck's side for a spell. He'll be able to help you."

"Many thanks, old friend," Cobb said.

"What are friends for?" Reeves asked.

Chapter 22

Heck Thomas

Stopping at night to ensure the horses and the pack mule were not overworked, the trip to Whitebead, Indian Territory, took about ten days and nights. The land wasn't harsh, but it was hilly in places. Wolf led the way, scouting ahead for dangers and good places to camp.

They reached Marshal Heck Thomas's office in Whitebead in the evening, around supper on the eleventh day. The extra day was due to Blaze's leg starting to limp slightly. They rested for a day, with Wolf rubbing Blaze's leg with an Apache liniment he always carried. The next day, the leg was fine, but they still moved more slowly.

The three detectives entered the Marshal's Office. Tasker spoke up, "Marshal Thomas, I assume?" He looked at a tall, lean man with dark eyes and a thick, drooping mustache. The man wore a simple flannel shirt, buttoned at the collar, and corduroy trousers tucked into knee-high boots. A distinctive quarter-moon and star badge, along with an ivory-handled, nickel-plated Colt revolver, signified his authority and made it clear to anyone that they should obey his commands. If that wasn't enough, a 12-gauge shotgun, similar to the one Cobb was rarely without, leaned against a corner.

"You must be Tasker, Cobb, and Wolf." His voice was firm and direct. As he said each name, he looked directly at them, one by one. His gaze behind those dark eyes was revealing – friendly but sharp. *A man who doesn't sugarcoat things*, thought Tasker.

Thomas continued, "I got a telegram from Judge Parker explaining your mission and asking me to give whatever help I can. He didn't have to ask. I've been after this Purdy bunch for a while, and I'm about to close in. I know where their wildcat whiskey still is located… down near Snake Creek."

Tasker asked, "Have you heard anything about our man, Turpin?"

"Not by name, but I hear rumors that Purdy has recruited about half a dozen new shooters. If I were a betting man — which I'm not — I'd wager a month's pay that your suspect is with Purdy. That's why I could use your help, not the other way around. They've got the numbers. Are you in?"

"I reckon so," all three nodded in agreement.

"Good. Burrell, Hank, Jim, get in here." Three men, all resembling Thomas in clothing and appearance, entered from the other room where the cells were located.

"I'm Burrell, Burrell Cox. Pleased to meet you." He opened the breech of his shotgun, emptied the shells into his hand, and hung it on two wall hooks.

"The second man said, "Call me Hank." He pulled up a chair, reversed it, and sat with his arms over the chairback.

The third man leaned casually against the door jamb and said, "I'm Wallace. Call me Jim. Howdy."

All three men projected competence and professionalism. "These are my deputies, Burrell Cox, Hank Childers, and Jim Wallace," Thomas said. "They'll be with us all the way." The Pinkertons introduced themselves as Thomas pulled out a large, folded map from a drawer and spread it on the desk.

"This is where we are now," he said, pointing to a spot on the map. "This is the still and cabin where Purdy and his fellow outlaws are holed up. We could rush in guns blazing, but they've got plenty of cover with the still, the cabin, and a couple of small outbuildings. Any ideas? I'd sure like to get them away from that hidey-hole."

As Tasker predicted, Cobb, his tactician, spoke up. He said, "How about this? See this cut he It seems to go through bits of high ground."

"It does," Thomas said.

"On each side of the road?"

"Yes."

"What if we lure them away from the still altogether and set up an ambush at the cut," Cobb suggested.

"How do we do that?" Cox asked. "First, how do we lure them out, and second, how do we ambush them with only seven men?"

The ambush is straightforward. I learned it from the Apache. Seven men with repeating rifles can take down fifty or more if we play it right. The goal is to trap them in a lethal setup. Guns will be firing from two sides at once, one from their flank and one straight ahead.

"Look," he pointed at the map. "You have a long stretch of road leading away from the still. It passes through a cut with a ridge on each side of the road. On both sides, the ridge is too steep for horses to climb easily. That means anyone in the cut can only go forward or back."

He paused to let that sink in, then continued, "Imagine the letter 'L' in your mind, with a long leg and a short leg. The long leg runs along the ridge, and the short leg crosses the road, blocking it. Between these legs along the road is a sort of 'box of death,' fired at on two sides."

"What do you mean by box of death?" Thomas asked, interested.

"Anyone caught in the box…is dead. Now, there are three men along the long leg on the ridge. Two more men are blocking the road at the short leg. One man is positioned along the road from the still, a bit before the cut."

"That's only six men," Childers said.

"The seventh man is at the still. His job is to make sure the others follow him into the ambush. He'll ride through the death box area, join the men on the short leg at the end, and become part of the blocking bunch."

"How the hell does he do that, and who's gonna take that job?" Thomas asked, glancing around the small office.

"That would be me," Wolf signed, cutting in. *"It's what I do, and I have no doubt I have the fastest horse."*

Cobb translated, then said, "Tell them how, Snip."

"I'll sneak in, set fire to the cabin in the back, then mount up. As they come out, I'll fire at them, giving them time to saddle up if they aren't already. Then I'll ride straight for the cut. They will follow. You boys will be alerted as I pass through the cut, then I'll stop at the end of the cut, turn around, and wait to block them."

When Cobb finished translating Wolf's signing, Thomas asked, a bit skeptical, "Can he do all that?"

"And more," Tasker said.

Cobb continued. "So, the men on the short leg block the road ahead for the outlaws. As soon as they're stopped in the death box, the men on one side of the ridge open fire on them. They can't retreat up the other side because it's too steep. If they try to escape back toward the still, the man waiting there on the road will discourage them. They're trapped."

There was a long silence as everyone considered the plan.

Cox said, "Sure beats runnin' in there head-on and takin' 'em out piece by piece, like a damn dentist."

Childers and Wallace nodded. Wallace said, "It'll be a turkey shoot … if it works."

Tasker said, "Cobb, Wolf, and I will take the short leg, if that's jake with you, Marshal?"

Thomas said, "And Cox, Childers, and I will take the ridge. Wallace, you take the position that allows them to pass, then cuts off any retreat back toward the still." Cox and Childers nodded.

Wallace said, "I'd love to."

Thomas said, "One more thing. When the short leg opens fire to stop them, I want you to fire high.

"Why, Marshal?" Tasker asked.

"I want to give them a chance to surrender – to drop their guns and come in peacefully."

"They'll likely be thirty or more, and we'll lose the element of surprise," Tasker said.

"I know, but that's the way it's gonna be, understand?"

"It's your show," Tasker said, "but I believe it's a mistake."

Thomas said, "That's it. We'll meet at first light here. Bring plenty of ammunition."

Later at the hotel bar, Cobb asked Wolf, "You ready for this, Snip?"

"As the saying goes – Born ready," Wolf signed.

"Tasker lifted his glass, "A toast." Cobb and Wolf raised theirs. "To getting this bastard Turpin." They drank, then went to their room.

Chapter 23

Showdown at Snake Creek

The posse hunkered down along Snake Creek, half a mile from the still. Wolf moved forward to check out the still and get an idea of how many outlaws were there.

Wolf moved slowly and steadily toward the still. He found a good spot with a clear view of the cabin, the two outbuildings, the still, and even the privy behind the cabin. The outlaw's horses were tied nearby, all saddled and ready in case they had to leave quickly. He was close enough to hear the outlaws talking, so he had to lie perfectly still. The conversations he overheard from various outlaws as they wandered about were of no use. They spoke only of food and women.

I count 19 horses. Where are the rest? Wolf waited, motionless, for several hours, then quietly moved to where Wind was patiently waiting, several hundred yards away.

"Everything looks as it did on the map," Wolf signed to Tasker and Thomas. *"I even rode through the cut. Our folks are hunkered down well out of sight. The numbers at the camp*

seem light. I waited several hours, and no one came out of the camp or went in. I counted 19 horses. I saw a few men coming in and out of the cabin and the outbuildings, mostly going to the privy. They looked like pistoleros — a mix of Gringos and Mexicans."

"Maybe our information was wrong. Could be only the nineteen," Thomas said. "Doesn't matter. We go with what we've got."

Tasker felt an increasing sense of unease, but he did not object. "When?" he asked.

"We'll set up the ambush at first light. Once we're ready, Wolf can go in."

Thomas gathered the posse. "No fires, cold meals, horses stay saddled, and no noise tonight. We leave at dawn." Nods all around, and each man went to his bedroll.

"What's wrong?" Wolf asked in sign. The three Pinkertons lay close together.

"Nothing, why?"

"I know you, Caleb. What's eatin' you?"

"I see it too," Cobb whispered.

"It's something. Maybe jitters, but something. I don't know. Hell, I'll get over it by morning. Go to sleep."

Dawn broke, and they put the plan into motion. The posse moved to the cut and found their positions. It took about an hour to build suitable cover for everyone. Cobb walked along the road, inspecting the ridgeline and the short-leg positions. When he was certain that no one could be seen from the road, he informed Thomas, who then sent Wolf on his way to the still.

Wolf circled around to approach the back of the cabin. He tied Wind to a hidden branch and crept forward, passing the privy to reach the back wall. No one was outside this early. He had plenty of time to gather wood from the nearby pile, build a fire, and light it. He ran back to Wind, rode around to the front of the cabin, and waited inside the woods for cover.

It didn't take long for the fire to burn down the cabin and force its inhabitants to flee. Other men in the outbuildings came outside to see what was happening. As Wolf had guessed, they initially thought it was an accident. Wolf waited until most of the outlaws were out in the open before he began firing the Winchester he had borrowed from Tasker. He knew he hit several of the men scrambling around, and their return fire into the woods was wild.

When he judged the right moment, he mounted Wind and charged out of the woods into the open, firing his pistol. Wind sped down the road toward the cut as the outlaws mounted their horses and gave chase. The plan was working.

At the cut, the posse heard the shots and prepared for their part. They heard the thunder of hooves before they saw Wolf galloping flat out toward them. He fired his pistol behind him as he rode at full gallop to the far end of the cut. Wolf pulled sharply on Wind's reins, stopping the horse as he slid off. He smacked Wind's rump, and the horse moved off into the wooded area beside the road. Wolf reloaded Tasker's Winchester and his Colt.

Tasker heard the hoofbeats grow louder as Wolf reached their position. The outlaws rode into the cut, still firing from horseback, apparently at the 'ghost' of Wolf, who was no longer there. Tasker, Cobb, and Wolf fired at the same time, over the heads of the mounted bandits, as Thomas had ordered. Their gunfire caused the outlaws to pull up and stop firing, leaving them confused for a moment. Their horses milled about on the road. They did not seem to have a leader.

Thomas shouted from the ridge, "This is Heck Thomas, U.S. Marshal! You're surrounded, and you don't stand a chance! Surrender, and you'll live! Fight, and you'll die! Your choice!"

As Thomas finished his last words, Wind ran out of the woods and across the road at a full gallop, whinnying. An unexpected burst of gunfire erupted behind where Wind had just crossed the road. The shooting was aimed at Tasker, Cobb, and Wolf. The ten or more outlaws who had been missing from the still charged down the road, firing as they advanced. The three Pinkertons spun around and returned fire.

The lead rider of the charging outlaws waved the others forward. Tasker thought it was Purdy. He still held Wolf's Springfield rifle. With one shot, he hit the man square in the chest. Several of the approaching outlaws were knocked from their horses in the Pinkertons' first volley.

The outlaws trapped below the ridgeline quickly realized help had arrived and opened fire on Thomas and his posse. The posse returned fire, and the air filled with gunsmoke and lead. Men on the ridge fired from cover at the outlaws, who were in the open, mounted, and mostly shooting wildly.

The slaughter ended in a few minutes. The outlaws lay on the road within the cut, either dead or badly wounded. Some had multiple gunshot wounds. Heck Thomas was also wounded. The three Pinkertons emerged unscathed and had killed all their attackers. The leader was indeed Aaron Purdy.

Turpin was wounded in both legs and was trying to crawl out of the area when Tasker and Cobb found him. They identified him from the Carte de Visite that Antonelli's policeman had found in Turpin's mansion. When the dust settled, the Purdy gang was gone, and the Pinkertons had their man.

Chapter 24

Confirmation of Suspicion

"Bring him in and put him in the back cell," Thomas ordered. Deputies Cox and Childers dragged Turpin through the Marshal's Office into the back room, where a row of cells lined one wall. They took him to the last cell, dropped him on the single cot, locked the door, and left. The other captured gang members, those still alive, already occupied the remaining cells.

A short while later, a doctor summoned by Thomas tended to the wounds on Turpin's legs. He emerged from the cell smiling. He reported, "Both wounds are no doubt painful, but not that serious. You can talk to him. Hell, with a few days' rest and some crutches for a time, he'll be as good as new."

"Thanks, Doc," Thomas said. He, his deputies, and the three Pinkertons were in the marshal's office, hashing out the day's events. Thomas turned to Tasker, Cobb, and Wolf. "First, my thanks to you boys for your help. Damned if that wasn't a fight. Jefferson, your plan was somethin' to see."

"It almost didn't work," Cobb said. "We didn't expect the

other half of the gang to be out of camp that morning or to hit us from behind."

Tasker asked, "Were you able to find out where they were?"

"Yeah," Deputy Wallace said, "One of them talked. That group had gone to Fort Sill to pick up supplies. They were on their way back when they heard the ruckus."

Tasker said, "Best laid plans."

Deputy Cox said to Cobb, "Those Apaches taught you well."

Cobb said, "I learned the hard way."

"What do you mean by the hard way?" Thomas asked.

"It was me in that death box, and the Apaches were in front and along a ridge. We were lucky to get out of it."

"I see what you mean. We chopped them up somethin' fierce. How did you manage to get out of it, Jefferson?"

Sammy Wolf was chuckling in a corner of the office. He had heard it all before, many times, and knew what was coming.

"That was Caleb, here," Cobb said, looking at his friend. "He was our Captain—10th Cavalry. We were getting slaughtered, losing men fast. I heard Caleb as clear as a mountain stream. I'll never forget it."

"What did he say?" Thomas and his three deputies hung on Cobb's words.

"Not much."

"What?"

"He said three things: "The hell with this! Follow me! Charge!" And we did. Those of us who were left followed that crazy bastard right up that steep ridge and straight at those Apaches. They were so shook they started runnin', and that's all she wrote. I'm here to tell the tale."

"What a story!" Thomas exclaimed.

Tasker spoke up, a big grin on his face. "You know, Sergeant Major, that's not quite the way I remember it. See, I recall saying all that crap and charging, yes, but I also recall that only a few followed me… at first. Then I heard this booming voice shouting something like "Get after the Captain, you bastards, or I'll feed yer dumb asses to the buzzards!" and that's when they all followed me. That booming voice was you, Sergeant Major. I also recollect that afterward, in camp that night, after thinking over how stupid I'd been, I went behind my tent and threw up – that's what I recall." By now, Cobb was grinning too.

Thomas said, "Well, it's one hell of a story, either way."

The deputies nodded in agreement.

"I guess you fellas would like a shot at Turpin," Thomas said.

"You bet we would," Tasker replied. "When?"

"Now's as good a time as any. I'll go along if you don't mind."

"Not at all." Tasker had one more task before the interrogation. He pulled Wolf aside. "Wolf, you've been invaluable in this assignment. Cobb and I are right proud of you, but I believe you're needed elsewhere."

He took a piece of paper from his pocket. It was a telegram from Doctor Abbott. Wolf was beginning to worry. He signed, *"Caleb, is it Savannah?"*

"Yes, but not in a bad way, I think. I'm not quite sure how to handle this."

"For God's sake, Caleb, what is it?" Wolf practically shouted, his hands raised.

Cobb moved closer to where they stood. "You'd better tell him," he said to Tasker.

"Tell me what?" Wolf demanded.

"About to do so." Tasker placed his hand on Wolf's

shoulder. "Doc Abbott says Savannah's with child. He's not mad, God knows why, but he thinks you need to come 'home,' his words, as soon as possible."

"When did you get this?" Wolf signed, angrily.

"Cox brought it about ten minutes ago. Go by train, Sammy. It's faster. Put Wind in the livestock car. I'll cover the cost."

Wolf paused for nearly a minute while Tasker and Cobb waited for him to absorb the news.

Finally, Wolf signed, *"I'm worried. I'm happy, but I'm worried. What must Doc and Mavis think of me?"*

Cobb said, "They love you, Snip. They want you as their son. They want Savannah to be happy. Nothing else matters. Go!"

They put Wolf and Wind on the first train out. Wolf left, waving goodbye as the train pulled away. He was smiling like the Cheshire Cat in Alice in Wonderland.

Turpin lay on the cot in his cell as Tasker, Cobb, and Thomas entered. He might have been a criminal mastermind or a New York tycoon, as he appeared in the Carte de Visite, but he had now lost his luster. He wasn't as tall as the picture suggested, and dressed in less than gentlemanly attire, he looked more like a worn-down cowhand. He wore a workman's shirt and trousers, both covered in trail dust. He had no hat. His hair was unkempt, and the sharp eyes that shone in the picture now looked dull and brooding.

Turpin could see their badges, so introductions were unnecessary. As they had arranged beforehand, Marshal Thomas began the interrogation. "I want you to know how lucky you are, Turpin. I have many charges I could bring, and you would most likely be convicted at a trial before Judge Parker in Fort Smith. You've heard of him, I'm sure—that's 'Hanging Judge Parker'."

"I've heard of him," Turpin said. He looked and sounded resigned to his fate. 'So how does that make me lucky?"

"These are Pinkerton men," Thomas said. "They've recently come from New York, where they compiled an impressive volume of evidence against you for multiple crimes. I think Judge Parker will agree to let the Pinkertons take you back to New York in chains to face your crimes. You're fortunate because if it were up to him, Judge Parker would likely hang you. In New York, they might show more leniency. That is, if you're willing to confess to your evil deeds both here and there."

"I'm not admitting to anything. Do your worst."

It was Tasker's turn. "We thought you might take that path, Turpin, so we brought you an incentive." He pulled out a satchel containing the evidence from the New York interrogations and searches.

"Here's what we know," Tasker said. "Based on eyewitness statements under oath and numerous incriminating documents — some bearing your name and many signed by you — we know you orchestrated a criminal ring with branches in New York and Chicago, extending to towns across the Western states and territories. We also know that you and your organization kidnapped young boys and girls off the streets of New York and Chicago, tortured them, and sold them into slave labor and prostitution out West. Furthermore, we have strong evidence linking you and your gang to homicides in both New York and Chicago. Our evidence indicates that you shipped bodies to pig farms out West to hide the crimes, far from where they occurred."

As Tasker laid it out, Turpin's face turned pale and pasty, but Tasker wasn't done. He was just getting started. From the satchel, he began pulling out samples of statements and documentary evidence. The more he showed Turpin, the more nervous and uneasy the alleged New York kingpin grew.

Tasker finally said, "We can put you so far in prison they'll have to pump sunlight into you, that is, if they don't hang you."

They watched his face twist and his eyes burn. He nearly shouted, "It wasn't me, damn you! I was under orders, you damn fools. I..."

Then he seemed to realize what he had said and stopped speaking. The lawmen in the room were stunned.

"What do you mean by orders, Turpin? What the hell are you talking about?" Thomas asked. They waited for an answer.

Turpin was silent for a long time. Then he seemed to brighten up, to gain new resolve. Some color came back in his face. He said, "I'm not taking this all alone. There are bigger fish. People you can't touch. People who'll have your asses. People who'll get me off. See, I won't hang. No, not me. You better believe it. You'll be the ones in trouble."

Cobb chuckled. "So, you think you have a hook, someone back East, who'll somehow set you free. No chance, Turpin. We have you beat, no matter how high your clout goes."

"No, no. It's not gonna happen."

A bell went off in Tasker's head. *I'll be damned. He's thinking he's protected by somebody on high.*

He looked at Cobb and whispered, "You thinkin' what I'm thinkin'?"

"If it's about somebody big in New York, I am," Cobb whispered back.

Tasker stood up, walked over to where Turpin sat on his cot. He slapped him hard across the face, then leaned in. "Listen, you little snake, you can't be thinkin' that lowlife senator's gonna help a toad like you?"

Turpin jerked his head back on hearing this.

Tasker continued now that Turpin had revealed a weak

spot. "We've got Senator Swane by the balls. We had him before we tracked you down. You'll be able to chat in the prison food line before they hang you both."

Turpin's demeanor changed. His facial features contorted, he began blinking constantly, sweat appeared on his forehead, and a twitch appeared below his left eye.

Heck Thomas, fascinated by Turpin's reaction, was completely in the dark. Cobb motioned him out of the cell and out of earshot. He said, "This Senator Swane was helpful when we were in New York, too damn helpful. Left a real bad taste. Tasker played a hunch using his name, and it paid off. You saw his reaction. I think we've got him now. He thinks we have Swane, which we don't, but he's going to give him to us. Watch and see."

Back in the cell, Tasker read the change in Turpin for exactly what it was. He bore in. "You've only got one choice. Give us Swane, and the court might go easy on you. That's it. No other choice."

"No way. I'd be d-dead meat."

"It won't happen. The government will protect you," Tasker said.

It was clear Tasker had struck a nerve, but it took another two hours to persuade Turpin to testify. Once he agreed, he began talking like a man possessed. He wouldn't shut up. Finally, Tasker had him sign a full confession in his own handwriting. He even provided the names of people, mostly fellow criminals, whom the organization had killed for various reasons and arranged for the bodies to be sent out west for disposal. It was everything— all the Western contacts, all the Chicago contacts, and all those in New York.

Tasker, Cobb, and Thomas traveled by train to Fort Smith. The marshal and the two Pinkertons appeared before Judge Isaac Parker, who deputized Tasker and Cobb to escort

Turpin back to New York. He also swore Turpin in and had him testify under oath about everything in the written statements Tasker had obtained. According to Turpin, he was merely the front man for a larger, more sinister plan organized by Swane and a small group of his henchmen.

Before leaving Fort Smith, Tasker and Cobb discussed their situation. Tasker began, "This is getting too damned big, Jefferson. We can't take this responsibility on ourselves. We can't trust anyone in New York, except maybe Lorenzo's coppers, and even they have their limits. Plus, they think the sun rises and sets on Swane. They might be tough to convince that he's crooked. If a US Senator is involved, we have no idea how high this goes."

Cobb said, "Bringing in Antonelli could threaten his career and those of his fellow officers. As crooked as his colleagues are—and with Tammany Hall backing them—it could cost them all their jobs, or worse. You know I'm pretty good at tactics, like setting up ambushes and the like, but this is way over my head."

"I'm thinking," Tasker said.

"Always dangerous," Cobb joked, "often means I'll have to shoot somebody or somebody will be shooting at me."

"Let's hope not. We don't have any authority in New York." Tasker fell silent for a moment. Both of them remained lost in their thoughts.

Tasker said, "We can present Turpin to the New York authorities, along with all our evidence and his confession, but we have no idea how they'll respond. They could simply destroy the evidence and either kill Turpin or let him go, likely the former."

"It's like putting our heads in the lion's mouth," Cobb said.

They went up to their room and had a couple of warm

beers they bought from the hotel bar. Sleep didn't come to Tasker. He lay awake for hours. At 3:00 am, he woke Cobb.

"Jefferson, we need to go see Will Pinkerton himself. I'll ask him to come from Chicago. We'll haul Turpin along, lock him up in the Albuquerque Headquarters holding cell, and meet with Will in person. We'll plan our next move with him."

"Best plan I've heard. Besides, I could use a little rest at the ranch before we jump into the lion's den."

"Let's get started."

It took a few days by train from Fort Smith to Albuquerque, where they locked Turpin in a holding cell at Pinkerton Headquarters. Before meeting William Pinkerton, they stopped at the ranch house, looked after Blaze and Two-Sock, and freshened up.

They had set Pinkerton up in a private office at headquarters. He sat behind a large desk. He had brought his two Gordon Setters from Chicago, and they sat on each side of Pinkerton's chair, guarding their master.

"When I received your telegram requesting a meeting here in Albuquerque," Pinkerton said, "I took the liberty of calling Lorenzo Colonna from New York to attend."

Tasker said, "Glad you did. Howdy, Lorenzo."

"Good to see you," Cobb added.

"Same," Colonna said, then asked, "You actually have Turpin locked up at our headquarters?"

"We do," Tasker said. "He's not too happy, but he sang like a canary."

"I know,' said Colonna. "I read his statements. You've definitely got him by the short and curlies. Nice work."

"What's happened in New York since we left?" Cobb asked.

"You stirred up a hornet's nest, all right. You definitely

dismantled the gang and their operations. When it went public, the politicians were forced to bring the culprits your Special Police Team had arrested to trial. Sentences varied, but as expected, they weren't too harsh."

Pinkerton added, "Same applies in Chicago, by the way. Nice work again. Jimmy O'Connor sends his regards. And let's not forget that Abigail is in her new home, safe and sound."

Tasker summed it up. "So, I take it 'missions accomplished,' but not 'case closed.' We still have two loose ends, Turpin, and the biggest and most important fish, Swane."

"That's my measure of it," Pinkerton said, "and they're a prickly pair – no pun intended. Any ideas?"

Tasker looked at Cobb, who nodded.

Tasker said, "Well, Will, we've been thinking about it quite a bit on our way here. It depends on how far you're willing to go to take down Swane."

"How do you mean?" Pinkerton asked cautiously.

"We have Turpin, with a mountain of evidence against him. I don't think even the crooks in New York could get him off, that is, if they wanted to, which I doubt."

Colonna said, "I agree on both counts. We have enough, but the corrupt politicians would rather see him dead than face trial. Otherwise, they can't stop it."

Tasker continued, "I think we also have the evidence against Swane, but he will have the full backing of the crooked politicians in Tammany Hall, probably because he has something on many of them."

"Again, I agree," said Colonna.

"Nonetheless," Tasker said, "Swane is the real enemy, the main bastard behind these horrible crimes, and he remains free, protected by political power and influence. We believe that bringing him to court would be a waste of time and could put everyone at risk, including us and, more importantly, the Pinkerton Agency itself. So again, the question is how far are we willing to go?"

Pinkerton nearly choked on the big cigar he'd been smoking since the meeting began. Colonna simply smiled, stood, and walked to the door. He opened it, looked down the hall in both directions, closed and locked it, then returned.

"Nobody here but us folks," said Colonna.

Pinkerton regained his composure. His eyes narrowed as he stared at Tasker and Cobb in silence for at least a minute. Tasker thought, *He's gonna fire us on the spot.*

When he spoke, his voice was soft and nearly inaudible. "Gentlemen, this conversation stays in this room. Do we understand each other?"

"Yes, sir," Colonna said. Tasker and Cobb nodded in assent.

He looked at Tasker and Cobb again and said, "I'm authorizing you two gentlemen to turn Turpin over to the New York police authorities. Then I want you to destroy Senator Swane, alive if possible, using any means you see fit, but without formally involving the police or any official organization. I want him to be unable to continue his criminal corruption activities within any part of our government for good. I understand this departs from my original orders. I can provide this assignment in writing if you wish. Do I make myself clear?"

Realizing their mission had escalated to a much more dangerous and politically sensitive level, Tasker said, "You do, perfectly clear, and we don't need anything in writing."

"Absolutely," Cobb echoed.

They stood to leave. Colonna followed. As he unlocked the door, Tasker turned and said, "We'll be in touch."

Chapter 25

Return to the City of Corruption

"I have an idea, especially since we know the New York gang might try to stop us," Tasker said, but he wouldn't elaborate. Cobb knew better than to press him.

Tasker contacted Mr. Clarence Pembrook by telegram and requested a favor. Pembrook quickly agreed. Tasker then, through Buford Cartwright, reached out to William Barstow Strong, President of the Atchison, Topeka, and Santa Fe Railway, and to Chauncey M. Depew, President of the New York Central Railway, both of whom were major clients of the Pinkerton Agency. The rest was straightforward.

Tasker and Cobb arrived at the train depot in Albuquerque to board the prearranged private train bound for New York City. It consisted of an engine, a tender, a first-class Pullman sleeping car, and a caboose. It was one of the newer engines and was rumored to be very fast. The crew included two engineers and a conductor. There were no other passengers.

Tasker wore a smug expression, while Cobb looked as if his eyes were about to pop out of his head. "Caleb, you never cease to amaze me. How in the name of all that's holy did you pull off this little stunt?"

"Easy," Tasker said. "I called in a favor from Clarence Pembrook and asked Buford to handle the rest. The A, T, & SF was happy to let us have our own train as a favor to the Pinkerton Agency, as long as Pembrook was willing to cover the costs, which he was—no questions asked."

"Do we have the entire train to ourselves?"

"Yep, at least to Chicago, with eight Pinkerton guards as escorts—two with the engineers, two at each end of our car, and two in the caboose. The guards will take turns sleeping all the way to the Windy City."

"What happens then?"

"We transfer to the New York Central line in Chicago. They were a bit less accommodating, but still willing to help. We'll have an escort, but only four men. We'll be in a first-class passenger car with a few other travelers, not in a sleeper. We'll station two guards at each end of the car, sleeping in shifts again."

While they enjoyed their new accommodations, the Guards led Turpin to the train. He was shackled hand and foot and moved with the typical prisoner's hop.

He was chained to a seat in the Pullman car, leaving him no room to move. One of the guards had to unchain him and escort him to the privy at the back of the Pullman. He looked surly but said nothing. He spoke very little during the entire trip to Chicago, which took several days.

Tasker and Cobb played cards, read, enjoyed the scenery, or slept while a guard kept watch over Turpin. Overall, the trip was comfortable.

That changed dramatically when they reached Chicago. They had to switch stations, and the New York Central Line was crowded, even in first class – not what they expected.

There were three other passenger cars in addition to the first-class coach. They had four first-class seats facing each other. Turpin was shackled to two of the seats, while Tasker and Cobb sat across from him in the other two. The remaining seats in the car were filled with passengers. Two Pinkerton guards sat together at each end of the car. Tasker, Cobb, and Turpin were seated roughly in the middle. Not only did the escort guards sleep in shifts, but Tasker also thought it wise for him and Cobb to do the same.

Trouble erupted on their first night out of Chicago. Cobb and Turpin slept while Tasker, wide awake, read a newspaper he'd picked up at their last stop. His first warning came when he saw six men crowd through the passenger car door at the front of the train. They paused there, watching the passengers, then quickly moved behind the unaware guards. They stabbed both Pinkerton men in their seats and then advanced single file down the aisle.

Tasker, who was sitting nearest the window, jabbed an elbow into Cobb's ribs, jolting him awake, then drew his Colt. The first man had a knife and looked straight at Tasker. The others, their guns drawn, seemed unsure of their bearings. Tasker drew both his Colts. As he did so, he saw the still-chained Turpin struggling to squeeze himself under his seat. Tasker's guns barked twice. The first two men went down, falling on top of seated women passengers. The women and some men screamed in panic. The other outlaws fired several shots. By now, Cobb was returning their fire. Clouds of white smoke from the gunfire in the tight space obscured everything.

Tasker fired both Colts, one after the other. He felt a sharp pain in his right shoulder. His right arm fell to his side, and the Colt in that hand dropped to the car floor. His right arm was useless. He kept firing the Colt in his left hand.

The Pinkerton guards at the back of the car were down, either wounded or dead, but the danger seemed to be coming exclusively from the front of the car. Cobb and Tasker kept firing until their Colts were empty.

A deafening silence fell as the white smoke settled. They saw that one gunman remained. Wounded and clutching his stomach, he was about to fire, slowly raising his gun, when Cobb fired three shots, hitting him in the head and chest. Tasker looked at Cobb, who held his empty Colt in his left hand and the smoking .38 pocket pistol in his right.

"You good?" Cobb asked.

"I'll live," Tasker said, holding his shoulder.

"How about you?" Cobb asked Turpin, who was slowly disentangling himself and crawling out from under the seat.

"You fellas are crazy. You're gonna get me killed."

"You're not dead yet," Cobb said. "I asked if you were hit."

"I'm not, but no thanks to you."

"You're welcome...asshole," Tasker said, awkwardly retrieving the Colt from the car floor and reloading both his revolvers. Cobb did the same with his Colt and his pocket pistol.

"I knew you were out, Jefferson. So was I. That tiny little thing came in damn handy."

"It did. I think I'll keep it handy. How's the shoulder?"

"Sore and numb, but no hole. Hit the whiskey flask in my upper-right vest pocket. Didn't go through, but it felt like I'd been hit with a sledgehammer. The pain's starting to fade." He flexed his shoulder and grimaced.

The passengers initially talked loudly, then gradually settled down. A few were hit by stray bullets in the tight space of the car, but luckily, their injuries were minor. One passenger was a doctor who treated the others' wounds. He examined Tasker's bruise and said he just needed to rest that arm for a while.

All four of their Pinkerton guards were dead. The two at the front had their throats slit, and the two at the back were shot dead by the gunmen. Cobb counted eight dead gunmen in the aisle.

Things were calming down. People returned to their seats, and in fact, the train had not come to a complete stop throughout the entire incident.

"These fellas are serious," Cobb said.

"They are," Tasker said.

Turpin added, "I think I mentioned that several times."

"So you did," Tasker said. "I guess you know they weren't after us. They want you dead."

"I'm gonna deny all those statements I made," Turpin said.

"You might try that," Cobb said, "but it wouldn't do much good. They'd still want you dead."

"God damn it!" Turpin said, his teeth clenched. He stayed silent.

About three hours later, as things were normalizing in the passenger car, a tall man with the brim of his slouch hat pulled low over his eyes stood from his seat near the front of the car and made his way toward the rear. Cobb, sitting in the aisle seat, felt uneasy. He didn't like the man's look, so he moved the small pistol from his pants pocket to his lap.

The man saw Cobb's move. As he walked by, he said, "Going to the privy." Cobb nodded.

Minutes later, a shot rang out over Cobb's left shoulder. A black hole appeared in Turpin's forehead, and his head jerked back before his body slumped forward. Cobb and Tasker reacted quickly, but it was too late for Turpin. When Cobb turned left after hearing the shot, the assailant was already running toward the rear car door. It was the man in the slouch hat.

Cobb chased him, with Tasker close behind. The gunman opened the passenger car door and ran onto the platform between the car and the caboose. The conductor was stepping out of the caboose when he ran into the man, who pushed him aside. The gunman was waving his gun at the off-balance conductor when Cobb shot him from behind. Once again, the little pistol did its job. The man in the slouch hat crumpled onto the platform, his gun flying out and off the train. His body was slowly sliding off the train as well.

Tasker joined Cobb on the platform and examined the conductor. He was dead, a bullet lodged deep in his chest. Cobb pulled the slouch-hat man back onto the platform. He was alive, but barely.

"Who sent you?" Cobb asked.

"Don't know. Never saw anyone." Cobb knew the man was bleeding too much and wouldn't last long in this world.

"I can save you," he said, "but only if you tell me who's paying you."

"Never saw 'em. Paid through a drop point... Help me."

"Too late, my friend. Too late." Cobb watched the man's eyes glaze over and his life seep out of him.

"Search his pockets," Tasker said. Cobb did so but found only a few .44 cartridges and a cheap pocket watch.

They returned to the coach to examine Turpin's body. Tasker said, "Well, that changes everything. Son of a ..."

Cobb checked the pockets of the other gunmen but found nothing. He also examined the faces of the remaining passengers seated on both sides of the aisle, carefully looking for any signs they might be shooters waiting to attack. Again, no luck. They appeared to be ordinary, well-dressed people traveling in a first-class coach.

Tasker said, "We need to get off this train before it reaches the station. They don't know Turpin's already dead, and they'll be waiting for us."

Cobb agreed, asking, "How? It's moving pretty fast."

Tasker and Cobb moved toward the first passenger car, behind the tender. They climbed onto the tender and into the compartment where two engineers were operating the train.

Tasker showed his badge. One of the engineers said, "They told us you'd be on the train with a prisoner. What's going on?"

"Prisoner's dead," Tasker said. "We need to get off before this train reaches the station."

"Can do," the engineer said, pulling the handle first to slow the train, then to stop it. "There's a town east of here. Small place. Just a few folks live there. Follow the creek bed over yonder." He pointed to a dry creek bed running parallel to the train.

As the train came to a stop, the engineer pointed to a shallow, meandering creek. Each carrying a carpet bag and their weapons, Tasker and Cobb jumped off the engine and vanished before the train started moving again.

The town was indeed small, with only a few houses, a general store, and a church – no saloon. The detectives went to the store and found a cheerful man named Nathan inside.

"We need to get to the city," Tasker said. "Maybe we could rent a wagon or two horses?"

"Nothing like that, Mister," Nathan said, "but we have one of them old-fashioned omnibuses that makes a run to the city every few days. It'll be heading there the day after tomorrow. You can pick it up right out front."

"Is there any way we could pay the driver to make an extra trip right now, like today?"

"Nah, he's pretty independent. I wouldn't even know

how to reach him. He shows up every few days."

"Great," Cobb said. "Do you have a place we could stay for a night or two?"

"No hotel or anything," Nathan said. "Not even a boarding house. We're just a stop on the road. We don't even have a name. But there's a small shack out back if you don't mind the clutter. There's a bed you can share, and you're welcome to eat with my family."

"Thanks. I reckon that'll be fine. How much?"

How does a dollar a day sound, includin' meals?

Tasker smiled and handed the storekeeper two silver dollars. When they were outside, he told Cobb, "We'll hunker down for two days and get into the city quiet-like."

"My very thoughts," Cobb replied. "They're going to find the body and know Turpin is dead."

"I know. Can't be helped. I wasn't about to drag it with us, and I just couldn't bring myself to throw the poor bastard off the moving train."

"How kind of you," Cobb said, grinning. "He was such an upstanding citizen, after all."

"*Pendejo*!" Tasker whispered. Cobb was now laughing.

Their days were pleasant. They dined with the storekeeper, his wife, and their two boys, ages eight and ten. The boys were fascinated by the Pinkertons' Western clothing, badges, and large guns. The storekeeper and his wife were friendly hosts, and she was an excellent cook. They nearly wished they didn't have to leave.

The omnibus was quite old, having gone out of fashion years ago. It was drawn by a single horse and had two benches, one on each side of the interior. The driver looked as old as the wagon but knew his job well. There were no other passengers that day.

The omnibus dropped them off in Upper Manhattan,

where they rented a Hansom cab to take them to Pinkerton Headquarters. Lorenzo Colonna was overjoyed to see them. "When the train arrived with Turpin's body and the dead fellas, we thought you were dead too. The engineers told us you got off, but then you didn't show. We thought they might have gotten you."

"They didn't," Tasker said.

"We can still try to go after Swane, but without Turpin's testimony, it's a toss-up at best. He's got some mighty powerful friends."

"So we heard," Cobb said, thinking that confronting this powerful politician who had stage-managed the trafficking ring would be far more dangerous than any previous enemy they had faced. Swane had vast wealth and significant influence. He also had a network of hired guns protecting him physically and a team of political loyalists shielding him from legal consequences.

He shared his thoughts with Tasker and Colonna, saying, "We need to think this through."

"Yeah," Tasker agreed. "Our frontier ways might not be enough in this jungle of corruption, but maybe a direct approach could work in our favor because they won't see it coming."

"That could be," Colonna said. "What do you have in mind?"

"I'm thinking, no search warrants, no police, no contact with anyone or anything that might alert Tammany Hall. We plan a raid on his mansion when we know he's there, using only Pinkerton men. Then we end him once and for all."

Colonna said, "I suspect that's what William Pinkerton was thinking when we met him. I like the concept. It's fighting fire with fire … but there's a long list of hazards in our way."

"Such as?" Tasker asked.

"First, we know there's a group of politicians cozy with Swane. I'd hate to see them start over once Swane is gone. Then there's the small army around him. At his house, he usually has local police hanging around, and he's fortified his home like a castle."

"How so?"

"He's hired members of a gang from Five Points called the 'Dead Rabbits' or the 'Roach Guards,' depending on which informant is squealing the loudest. They're not professionals, more like Irish thugs, but they're tough and no pushovers. Swane is supposed to keep them well-armed. Lastly, and I know this for a fact, there's no way we could keep Antonelli's team of Italian policemen out of this. In the end, they'll have to clean up the mess anyway."

"I see what you're saying, but isn't Antonelli close with Swane?" Tasker asked.

"He won't be once he sees the evidence you've brought."

Cobb said, "We could find a way to gather all his cronies at the mansion. As for his 'army,' we should be able to muster enough help to handle them."

Colonna said, "What about Antonelli? If he's on board, he could be crucial in identifying Swane's associates. Also, Swane's mansion is near Tarrytown, right on the Hudson River, outside the city. Antonelli might be able to keep the Tarrytown police away from us, that is, if they aren't already on Swane's payroll."

Cobb said, "I say bring Antonelli in. I think we can trust him. I'd rather have him with us than hear about it and risk him working against us."

Tasker nodded in agreement.

"Good," Colonna said. "Let's meet again in two days. I'll work on this meeting of the cronies and bring Antonelli to the next meeting. Let's do it here at Headquarters. It's safer."

Chapter 26

The Reckoning

As Colonna suspected, Antonelli and his Italian police squad wouldn't be left out of this operation. He was shown the evidence and simply said, "Son of a bitch!"

This time, he brought along—or at least called in—about 30 tough coppers eager for a chance to do the right thing. Additionally, Colonna brought 40 Pinkerton men, eager to leave their strike-breaking duties behind. No date was set for the assault, so they waited on standby. It was a formidable force.

Sergeant Antonelli told Colonna that he had a recent list of corrupt politicians in various positions within the New York City government. He had been collecting documents and witness statements for years, hoping that someday someone would do the right thing so they could arrest the entire corrupt group. There were about two dozen of them. What he had missed until now was that Swane was the mastermind.

Antonelli also knew that this shady group met every few weeks at a lavish party held somewhere outside the city. He was never able to pinpoint the exact location of the parties.

He used all the favors he could from various prostitutes

his men had recruited as informants over the years. Colonna did the same with his Pinkerton agents.

Now that they had Swane as a specific target, they identified the location of the parties as Swane's mansion on the Hudson River. This, of course, worked perfectly for the task force. As soon as the location was determined, Antonelli mounted discreet surveillance of the mansion, monitoring all comings and goings.

The key was now to determine when their next meeting was scheduled. That information did not come easily. In fact, obtaining it may have cost one of Colonna's best operatives his life.

A week later, Colonna called a hurried meeting with Tasker, Cobb, and Antonelli. He gave them a solemn report. "A few weeks ago, in anticipation of our ongoing investigation into this child abduction ring, I pulled one of my best operatives, and a good friend, Paul Withers, off his work infiltrating the Unions. He was solely focused on investigating what remained of this ring," he said.

"While trying to find out when the next meeting might take place, he visited a bar popular with members of the Dead Rabbits Gang. For no clear reason, one of the gang members took a dislike to Withers. He challenged Withers to a fistfight in the alley outside the bar. Withers was an ex-boxer, so I doubt he felt very threatened. He probably thought winning such a fight would win him favor with those in the bar. When Withers stepped outside through a back door, several thugs were apparently waiting. He was attacked and stabbed multiple times in the chest and back. They kicked him so violently that he was almost unrecognizable and left him dying, choking on his own blood. He was found by our men an hour later but died before they could get him to a hospital."

Tasker and Cobb said nothing, lost in thought over such a loss. Antonelli put his arm around Colonna's shoulders. Tasker broke the silence. "Lorenzo, we're so sorry. We know how losing one of our own hurts. Anything we can do?"

"Thanks, but no. Everything's been taken care of. We'll handle the arrangements and his family. I just wanted you to know the cost of the information I'm about to share and why I believe it's reliable."

Tasker, Cobb, and Antonelli nodded.

"Withers was murdered last night. Yesterday, he submitted a report detailing a meeting with one of his informants. His source, a prostitute, told him she had been invited to a big party at a mansion along the Hudson. The party is scheduled for next week. She has attended previous parties there and knows it is the home of New York Senator Swane. She described him as very handsome but a pig. She also mentioned that children occasionally attend the parties, but she assumed they were the children of the party guests."

Tasker asked, "Was this prostitute involved in Withers' death? Is she all right?"

"She wasn't involved. She's fine," Colonna said. "I don't think there's any connection between her giving information to Withers and his murder. As far as we know, she's safe, and we're still good. Thanks to Withers' fine work, we have the date of the next meeting between Swane and his cohorts."

"This is good news, but we also have a new wrinkle," Tasker said. "There might be kidnapped children at the mansion, which requires careful moves to avoid harming them."

"It does," Cobb said.

"We'll include that in the plan," Colonna said.

Antonelli nodded.

"What about the local Tarrytown police?" Tasker asked Antonelli.

"I'll send one of my men to the Tarrytown police station just before we raid. He'll persuade the locals that it's not in their best interest to get involved. If he doesn't succeed, we'll take care of it when the time comes."

Colonna asked, "What do we do about this so-called 'castle guard' of his?"

"We shout 'police' as we go in," Antonelli said, "and any resistance we meet will be overwhelmed by heavy gunfire!" They all smiled, then grew serious.

"Actually, we need the element of surprise, especially if they have children inside," Tasker said.

"That makes it tricky," Antonelli said.

Cobb said, "Let's use a battering ram to break through the door first and yell 'police.' Then we'll have to move fast."

'That's about all we can do right now," said Colonna. I'm trying to get the floor plans for his mansion. We should finalize the plan tomorrow night, then launch the assault the next night, during the party."

They all agreed.

The Swane estate resembled a fortress, with brick walls like those of a castle surrounding the property. The entire estate sat atop rocky formations at the edge of the Hudson River. A massive tower loomed over the large house and grounds. At the entrance, a set of ten-foot-tall carved mahogany doors stood. The only thing missing to make it a true medieval castle was a water-filled moat with alligators or man-eating fish. Colonna drew up a rough floor plan but couldn't guarantee its accuracy.

Antonelli brought several paddy wagons but parked them out of sight of the mansion. According to their final plan, the two assault teams moved in first. Tasker, Cobb, and Antonelli, along with the Italian squad of about thirty men, headed for the front doors, while Colonna's Pinkertons circled around to the back.

The front assault team began by smashing the large mahogany doors. As soon as they heard the crash at the entrance, the team at the back forced their way through the rear door. The guards at both the front and the back were shocked and immediately raised their hands, but not before sounding a loud siren that alerted everyone inside the castle. Two intense gunfights erupted as the assault units engaged guards on the mansion grounds, both at the front and the rear.

The party-going politicians and female escorts erupted into chaos, running every which way to escape the incoming gunfire. It was no use. Both entrances were sealed off.

Colonna was right; these defenders weren't professionals, but they were stubborn. There was no sign of Swane. Antonelli and Colonna, approaching from the front and back of the house, began the difficult task of clearing the mansion room by room, and there were many rooms. As they moved through, they rounded up members of the Dead Rabbits, politicians, and prostitutes, but still no sign of Swane or any children.

Tasker and Cobb allowed the assault teams to do their worst while they focused on finding Swane. When he wasn't in the main ballroom, they began searching less obvious rooms that others might have overlooked.

Cobb thought for a moment. "Caleb, hold on a second. Swane has turned this entire mansion into a castle, right?"

"He has, and …"

"Where would they keep prisoners in a castle?"

"Shit! Of course, in a dungeon."

Gunfire continued throughout the mansion, but Tasker and Cobb ignored it. They searched for a door or staircase that might lead them to a basement or dungeon. It felt like an eternity, but Cobb finally found a locked metal door. He used his shotgun to blow the lock. As soon as the door swung open, gunfire erupted from the bottom of a long staircase. Bullets chipped the walls and ricocheted off the metal door.

They both fired down the stairs, with Tasker's Winchester on the right side of the doorway and Cobb aiming his shotgun on the left. They kept firing until they heard footsteps quickly retreating. Cautiously but swiftly, they moved down the stairs. At the bottom was a long hallway carved into the stone beneath the mansion. At least two shooters were at the far end, firing wildly. They didn't shoot back but ran toward the gunmen. As Tasker and Cobb got closer, the shooters disappeared from view.

At the end of the corridor, another metal door stood slightly ajar. When Cobb nudged it with his shotgun, a burst of gunfire erupted from the other side, ricocheting off the door. As they listened, they could hear the faint cries of children's voices.

Cobb immediately moved as if to charge through the door, but Tasker stopped him by grabbing his arm.

"How many you figure?" Tasker asked.

"Too many," Cobb answered. "I'd say at least half a dozen. You hear that? There are children in there. Let's go."

By this time, three of Antonelli's coppers had joined them. One of them handed Cobb a round object with a fuse protruding.

"What the hell is this?" Cobb asked, eager to move.

"It's a grenade," the policeman said. "Light the fuse and throw it. It's a 3-second fuse."

Tasker grabbed the grenade from Cobb. He said, "When I throw, we go. Cobb and I will move right; you go left." There were now four policemen. They all nodded in agreement.

Tasker pulled a match from his vest pocket, struck it

against the stone wall, and lit the fuse. When he saw the fuse was halfway burned, he threw it into the room on the other side of the metal door.

The explosion was intense and effective. They stormed in, shooting as they advanced.

It was a large room with cells lining three of the four walls. Some cells held children, crying inside. Swane stood in front of them, a small girl before him, his arm around her neck. He pointed what looked like a large LeMat pistol at her head. Hired shooters — not the Dead Rabbit fools, but likely professionals, judging by the way they used cover and held their weapons — surrounded him. There were ten of them.

It was a standoff. The gunmen aimed at the police officers, and the officers aimed back, but no one fired.

"Senator Swane," Tasker said calmly, "there's no way out."

Swane shouted, "Shoot them, damn you, shoot them!"

These were professionals; they saw the odds, weighed their chances against what Swane was paying them, and left him wanting. One of them said, "We're done." The others lowered their guns.

Swane yelled, "Bastards!" He turned and ran through a nearby doorway, dragging the little girl with him. He slammed the large metal door shut, and they heard the lock click on the other side.

Tasker turned to the policeman who had handed him the grenade. "You take care of this bunch and see that the children get upstairs to safety. We're going after the little girl."

"Yes, sir," he replied.

Tasker tested the metal door that Swane went through, and, as expected, it was locked on the other side. He turned to the policeman. "You got any more of those grenades?"

"No, sir, sorry."

Tasker and Cobb hurried back to the door they had entered, dashed down the hallway, and climbed the stairs.

"Something's wrong, Caleb. I smell smoke."

Me too. You think that bastard planned to burn this place down if he was caught?

"Wouldn't put it past him."

Rooms were filling with smoke, and visibility was quickly diminishing. They hurried through a winding maze of hallways, checking each room along the way. They headed roughly toward the stairs they believed Swane had taken to reach the main part of the building. It was a risky guess. When they reached the main ballroom, they saw police guiding the children out onto the lawn. Flames were now visible in many areas of the mansion, including the ballroom ceiling. Smoke was rapidly thickening.

Cobb yelled, "The tower?"

Tasker shouted back, "No way. His own fire would trap him, with nowhere to run."

"Where then?"

As Cobb asked the question, they both spotted Swane across the ballroom, the little girl under his left arm, her feet swinging, and the big gun still in his right hand.

Tasker shouted, "Give it up, Swane!"

"I don't think so," he said, turning and running through another door.

The ballroom's roof was on fire, with flaming debris falling nearby. "We've gotta get out of here," Tasker said.

"Not without the girl," Cobb said. "I'm not leaving without that little girl."

Tasker shouted, "He's not trying to commit suicide; that door he went through should lead outside."

A charred, smoldering beam fell from the ceiling and struck Cobb. He collapsed beneath it, the beam resting on him. Tasker kicked it away with his boot and helped Cobb to his feet. Cobb was only partially conscious. The two detectives headed toward the large mahogany front doors, which stood open.

Outside, on the lawn between the tall walls and the blazing mansion, they found Colonna and Antonelli, with most of their teams still present. They were caring for the small group of traumatized children rescued from the mansion's inferno. Nearby, a group of gang members and gunmen sat on the lawn, handcuffed and guarded by police. There was no sign of Swane or the little blond girl.

Tasker asked Cobb, "Can you make it?"

Cobb replied, "I'll make it. I lost my shotgun."

"Yeah, my Winchester's toast by now, too. Let's find Swane."

They hurried around the mansion to the side where the door Swane used to escape from the ballroom should have been. They found it open. Not far away, along the outer wall, was another open door leading to a wooded area outside the mansion's inner grounds. They moved into the woods at a slow run.

"Alice in Wonderland," Tasker said.

"Yeah."

"That LeMat holds nine bullets and a shotgun shell," Tasker said.

"It does," Cobb replied. "We seem to be headed toward the river."

The wind was their enemy. Smoke from the raging mansion fire drifted through the woods, making it hard to see ahead and nearly sending them over a cliff overlooking the Hudson River. They stopped abruptly and looked around. Nothing was in sight.

"Could we have passed them?" Cobb asked.

A voice from the smoky haze said, "Stay where you are, gentlemen, and raise your hands."

The detectives followed the order. As the smoke cleared, Swane rose to his feet, gun in hand, about twenty feet away. The small blonde girl's body lay at his feet, still and silent. The fiery red glow from the nearby burning mansion reflected on Swane's face, giving him a ghostly, devilish look.

"What now, Swane?" Tasker shouted. "You're not a senator anymore, you're not a criminal mastermind anymore, and in fact, you're not much of anything anymore."

"And it's all your fault. You Pinkerton bastards. I had an empire!"

"'Had' is the right word," Cobb said. "An empire built on the blood of children you sold into a living hell. That little girl lying there—is she another of your victims? Is she dead, too?"

"No, but soon. First, I owe you two for all the trouble you've caused me." He fired once and hit Cobb in the stomach. Cobb fell backward to the ground and didn't move. Tasker, whose hands were still raised, started to reach for his gun. Swane stopped him, pointing his gun at the little girl. He said, "Don't try it, or she gets the shotgun shell." Tasker froze, looking back at Cobb, who lay still, bleeding from the stomach wound.

"You know, Tasker, I'm a superb shot. I've got trophies to prove it, or I did—now they're all gone. There's something I'm curious about, Tasker?"

"Are you gonna shoot me or talk me to death? You better kill me, Swane, or I'm gonna kill you."

"Are you as good with your left hand as you are with your right?" He shot a second time. This one hit Tasker in the right shoulder. He dropped his right arm to his side, clutching his right shoulder with his left hand. He thought, *Again, same place, worse this time?* Blood oozed through his fingers.

"Now I'm gonna let you watch while I fire the shotgun shell from this pistol into this pretty blond thing at my feet." He made a show of slowly adjusting his LeMat pistol's hammer selector pin downward to enable the shotgun barrel to fire. This distracted Swane for a second.

Tasker said, "I think not." He had already used his painful right hand to draw the small pistol from his right pants pocket, cock the hammer, raise his right arm with his left hand to aim, and fire. The .38 bullet created a tiny black hole above Swane's left eye. His head jerked, and he disappeared.

Tasker's trouser leg smoldered where the bullet and burning powder had passed through. Tasker patted the leg, which looked as if it might burst into flames, and made his way over to the blond girl.

First, he saw that Swane had fallen over the cliff edge, his head wound visible. It was about 200 feet to the rocks below. Then he saw that the little girl was alive, awake, and smiling up at him. He picked her up and carried her to Cobb's still form on the ground.

Antonelli burst through the underbrush and reached his side. Cobb slowly opened his eyes. He saw the girl beside him smiling. He saw Antonelli looking concerned. Finally, he looked up at Tasker and said, "Good, Caleb, you did good." Then he closed his eyes again.

Tasker remained silent, tears streaming down his face.

EPILOGUE

No, Cobb didn't die. It took nearly a year to recover, but he survived. However, he missed Sammy Wolf's wedding to Savannah Abbott. Cobb's recovery was aided by Sammy and Savannah's presence at the ranch in Albuquerque. She cared for him as she had cared for Sammy when he was wounded on a previous assignment in Serpent's Creek.

Tasker's right arm, having been hit slightly the first time and severely the second, nevertheless healed quickly.

They found Swane's body among the rocks. His political allies and his 'little army' were all arrested, either at the mansion or later at their homes, those still alive, that is. Even the Tammany Hall politicians couldn't protect them, and some of them went down as well.

Sergeant Antonelli was promoted to Lieutenant in the New York Police Department.

Abigail and Micky, now reunited, were happy in their new home with the Pembrooks.

Well, what of the little blonde orphan, whom Tasker and Cobb rescued from the cliff above the Hudson River and named Becky? She found a happy home with Dr. Tobias and Mavis Abbott.

As for Sammy Wolf-Killer, alias Samuel Wolf, he settled

down with Savannah as the well-respected Town Marshal of Serpent's Creek, New Mexico Territory, secretly hoping that Caleb and Jefferson would call on him again.

When he was fully recovered, Cobb rejoined Tasker for more adventures. After their success dismantling the Human Slavery Ring, they were asked by Judge Isaac Parker to leave the Pinkerton Detective Agency and become full-time Deputy U.S. Marshals… but that's another story.

THE END

About the Author

Passionate, riveting, with meticulous research - those are words reviewers use to describe the works of Will Hutchison. He is a retired military officer with two combat tours in Vietnam with the Marines, followed by many years as a CID Special Agent in the Army, and even more years as a Special Agent in the US Nuclear Regulatory Commission. After retiring from government service, he published three award-winning historical novels in *The Ian Carlisle Series*, covering the Crimean War (*Follow Me to Glory*), the American Civil War (*The Gettysburg Conspiracy*), and the Indian Wars period in the American west and Canada (*Satan's Last Whisper*). He has also completed two award-winning non-fiction historical and photographic works, one focusing on surviving artifacts of the Crimean War (*Crimean Memories: Artefacts of the Crimean War*), and the other on surviving artifacts of the Battle of the Little Big Horn (*Artifacts of the Battle of Little Big Horn: Custer, the 7th Cavalry & the Lakota and Cheyenne Warriors*). More recently, he authored the first installment of a trilogy set in the old West (*The Sins of Serpent's Creek*). This book, *Orphan Hunt*, is the second in this series.

Will Hutchison now lives in Gettysburg with his wife, Rosemary, and their Shetland dog Stormy, and devotes his time to writing, photography, and lecturing.

www.ingramcontent.com/pod-product-compliance
Lightning Source LLC
LaVergne TN
LVHW050629100826
845148LV00011B/1789